Battles of Azriel: Arya
# BOOK 2
# COLOURS WITHIN

## DANICA PECK

Colours Within

Copyright © 2017 Danica Peck



Published by Ouroborus Book Services via IngramSpark
www.ouroborusbooks.com.au

Cover design by Wayne Nichols
www.wnichols.com

Map by Amber Morant
www.ambermorant.com

Battles of Azriel

# COLOURS WITHIN

## Book 2: Arya

# DANICA PECK

Dedicated to my Alice in Wonderland girls.
I love you girls to the moon and back; and I'm
thankful every day that I found you all.

*'Maybe our girlfriends are our soulmates, and guys are
just people to have fun with'*
*– Candace Bushnell*

Visit Danica at:

www.facebook.com/danicapecknovels

Unclaimed Lands
Ghost Territory
Vampire Territory
Dark Elf Territory
Werewolf Territory
Underland
Alesmera
Ilyragasia
Meradom
Dragon Territory
Hollows
Mountain Falls
Kirravigne
Ucyenae
Mystique
Kierra
Robin Falls
Krypto
Versattali
Startex
Skarsgard
Alegesia
Meranique
Saberial
Katailita
Vila
Lyndittra
Azriel - the world of five kingdoms

# CHAPTER ONE

Arya's History

I was born as Arya Faith DeValentino and like every teenager, I went through a phase of not liking my name and was known as only Faith. This was timed perfectly as a supernatural war was just beginning. During this time, I made many enemies and ultimately, they came after me and my family. Most couldn't find us because of my change of name, but that was many moons ago.

I was born in 1905 and stopped aging at the age of sixteen. Yes, that is correct, eternity as a teenager. I'm lucky it was after the bad skin and the awkward looks stage of adolescence. I am the first of my species to be born. The rest of my siblings were made, from humans, into my father's species – Nagual. I am a hybrid; my Mother was a Minx and my Father the Nagual.

What's a Nagual? In less fancy terms, we were just shape shifters: and we turned into jaguars. We had basic magic that was connected to the Earth and when turned, a black cat mark appeared on our wrists.

And a Minx? They were just elves, well kind of. History says that an Elf and a Siren bore a child, which is how the first Minx was created. And that's what I am, a Minx with all the power qualities of a Nagual.

I may not be human, but I have made mistakes. I was an Elf with human regrets, an immortal with a mortal soul. My mistakes would haunt me till the end of days. I've watched my brother die. I've watched my fiancé die.

What do you do when, in your world, you can't die from old age? The only death in our world is murder.

What did I do? I let magic and revenge consume me.

I wished for a mortal life.

# CHAPTER TWO

Vila 1984

It was a surprisingly cold night for November. Perhaps it was the storm, which often brought the cold winds. The water that fell from the sky was like ice, but I didn't flinch. Perhaps my skin was now used to it, for it had been hours since I was standing in the rain in this run-down town.

Before the rain, before me, this town had been full of life. Now there were only the memories of pain and death. I looked over the destruction I had caused, but no emotion ran through me, no guilt or pain. Around me, the buildings that had been left standing began to sink deeper into the earth as the flames stole their last bit of strength. The wind carried the screams of the deceased, their blood stained the ground upon which I stood, despite the rains' best effort to wash it away.

As the remains of a building crashed into the wet dirt with a small cry, I turned my attention to it, as though expecting someone to emerge from the rubble.

My olive skin had a slight glow from the remaining flames, though most of my skin was hidden by the crimson essence of the departed. My skin revealed no wounds, even with the amount of blood that covered me it was hard to believe. Not even the rain could remove my sins. Tainted, red rain fell upon my lips but I didn't feel sickened by the rusted coin taste that found its way upon my tongue. My midnight hair fell past my elbows, sticking to my skin like a spider web. My onyx eyes glanced up at the moon; tonight was the night. I had waited long enough. I felt intoxicated with power and revenge, and this violated town was the ideal place to end my vendetta.

The cries of people watching someone they loved being murdered, the screams of terror and the ear piecing shrieks of the dying, echoed within my mind. The moon had broken through the clouds and cast its light over me as I waited. I waited for him – the one that had caused my suffering. Tonight it would end.

A twig snapped behind me. I smiled, exposing my feline teeth, as a dark, brooding figure walked towards me. I turned to face him, meeting his gaze. As he closed the space between us I looked him over. His dark brown hair fell around his face, his dark blue eyes shone out from his ghostly pale features.

'Jedhail,' I whispered, loathing rising within me. 'What better place to meet your demise.'

'Impressive,' he murmured with his velvety voice. 'I envy the fame you will receive.'

Hunger filled his eyes as he gazed over my body, still stained with red.

'I suppose you want to fight?' His voice had a sense of arrogance as he took a step back. 'But as my final words, may I tell you a bed time story?'

I went to snap my impatience at Jedhail but he put his hand up to interrupt me.

'This is the tale of murder and love, the story of your two significant others.'

'Why would I want your version of killing Rhys and Mikhail?' I shouted.

'Ah, that's why,' he mused. 'I didn't kill Mikhail.'

'That's a lie,' I argued, though my voice wavered with uncertainty.

'Are you sure?' he teased.

I thought back to Mikhail's death. He was right, I wasn't sure. I never saw his killer's face, I was too far away. But if Jedhail hadn't kill Mikhail, who had?

'The blame goes to me,' said a soft, sweet voice from behind Jedhail. Elphina, his partner, appeared – she was a spider demon, a rare pureblood demon species of vampires.

Spider demons are evil, full stop. Vampires can be swayed either way and that's how this power couple happened. Elphina seduced a young innocent-souled vampire, Jedhail, to give up his soul, he then became her own personal slave and puppet. He had no idea that he was just her tool.

'You?' I exclaimed in disgust, as Elphina walked towards me.

Blue electrical sparks flew from my fingertips as anger and hatred swelled within me.

'The amazing Faith,' Elphina mused as she walked closer to me. 'Or are you going by Arya again? Either way, Mikhail was luscious, wasn't he? I wish I had dug my claws in first.'

I threw myself at Elphina, who avoided the attack. I landed in a crouch position, a low growl coming from the back of my throat as rage began to consume me.

'Aw, baby,' Elphina mocked. 'You can't beat me.'

I smiled through my feline teeth, taking her words as a challenge.

I threw myself at Elphina again. This time she didn't react at the same speed causing her to almost lose balance. Elphina lashed out at me with her claws, I ducked the attack and spun a kick into her stomach. Elphina doubled over and glared at me as she caught her breath.

With a quick glance, I saw Jedhail circling us like a bird circling its prey. He had no motive to join the fight, so I put my focus back on the current target. I threw continuous attacks at Elphina, keeping her in the defensive position, not allowing her an opening to attack.

Elphina scrunched up her face in frustration, lashing her claws out against my neck. As I pressed my hand to the wound, Elphina took the opening and punched the side of my face. With the combination of the wet ground and the hit, I lost my footing and landed in the mud.

I quickly brushed off the hit and jumped back to my feet ready to attack again, but Elphina was quicker. She had drawn a titanium blade. She jammed the blade into my stomach so fast, I barely blinked. I was clenching her fist and holding in the urge to scream, falling to my knees. My hands grabbed the hilt of the blade.

Elphina kneeled before me, looking me in the eyes. 'Recognise the blade? It's the one I killed your lover with.'

*How could one person bleed so much?*

That had been the only thought that was going through my head as I had supported Mikhail's wound. That's all I could think about now. Elphina pulled on my hair, forcing my head back for our eyes to meet.

'You know Mikhail begged for his life?' Elphina snarled.

'You lie!' I spat.

'He screamed,' Elphina purred. 'He begged. He was pathetic.'

A low growl rose from my throat. I pulled the blade from my stomach and slashed it across Elphina's cheek. Throwing my hands forward I conjured a gust of wind which threw Elphina onto her back. I pushed myself to my feet and as Elphina stood up, I plunged the blade into Elphina's chest. She screamed in agony as I twisted the knife, opening the wound further. She fell to the ground and I watched as her spirit left her body.

Jedhail ran to Elphina's side as I stumbled backwards away from both of them.

'Raphael, Angel of Ease,' I whispered, my strength waning. I was on the verge of collapsing, but Jedhail still lived.

'Raphael...Angel of ...ease, in the divine ...name of...Raphael,' I murmured using all my strength to stay conscious. 'I consecrate and charge, I ask for healing, from the rain ...from the earth. Raphael...Angel of Ease.' A white light appeared and swirled into my wound.

Jedhail's cold, dark eyes were shooting daggers as he walked over to me while I was kneeling on the ground supporting my wound. Jedhail back-handed me, causing me to spit blood from my mouth.

'Kill me,' I snarled. 'I dare you.'

Jedhail licked his lips, showing his fangs. His eyes travelled from my neck to my eyes. He kneeled before me, grabbing my chin, forcing me to look at him.

'No,' he whispered, and smiled as disappointment flickered in my eyes. 'How does it feel *ma petite*, the vengeance? Was all the blood worth it?'

My onyx eyes glanced dangerously at him. 'I feel nothing.'

Jedhail scoffed.

I winced as I tried to stop the bleeding from my still open wound.

'Liar – what would Rhys say if he saw what you did here? What would Mikhail say?'

I looked at him, my eyes faded back to blue from black; the magic's hold on me relinquished, allowing the remorse and pain to all set in.

Jedhail smiled. 'Feel the pain, taste the blood,' he whispered coldly in my ear. 'Being the creature you are, I believe this will haunt you forever.'

Sensing the sunrise, Jedhail walked off leaving me in my despair.

# CHAPTER THREE

35 years later

The rain was falling more intensely tonight, as though the gods were taking their sides in this war that continued down on the land. The roads were all flooded so high that it was soon entering people's houses. I ran over the rooftops, jumping from roof to roof. My adrenaline racing, and my blood boiling beneath my skin. My subconscious silently hoping that I wouldn't slip and fall as the flowing water seemed to be against me.

As I reached the end of the rooftops in the neighbourhood, I jumped to the ground and ran through the trees. With the pouring rain and the moonless night, I was surprised that I could see anything. In the distance, I suddenly saw a light. I knew a fence to the yard was coming up so I jumped up into a nearby tree and climbed up to a stable branch. Once I caught my balance I jumped to the fence and down into the yard, landing on all fours.

As I stood up, a strike of lightning flashed across the sky reflecting my anger within, a deafening crash of thunder made the rain and my deep breaths sound silent.

The gravestones on either side of me didn't faze me; my gaze was focused on the light coming from within the church. I knew he was in there, I could sense him. As I reached the doors I pushed them open, a violent gust of wind broke into the church.

Jedhail didn't turn at my entry, he remained standing at the front of the church with his back to me. The candle light flickered from the wind.

'No point praying, he wouldn't answer you,' I mocked coldly.

Jedhail turned slowly around with a charming but cruel smile upon his lips. He flashed his fangs, sending shivers down my spine.

'There is more chance of the gods answering me,' he said as we both walked towards each other. 'I admit evilness. I embrace it. But you? You blink your eyes at how good you are but we both know you're as evil as I am.'

I smiled; the flames of the candles rose higher as though they could feel the heat in this moment.

In a single motion, too quick for the human eye to see, I had Jedhail pinned on his back with a knife to his throat. The blade was made from crystal and dead man's blood, a weakness to vampires. I saw a flicker of fear in his eyes but he hid it with a snarky comment.

'I don't feel your passion in this. Should we get naked and have you jump me that way?' he said before he kicked me off. We both jumped to our feet but he was faster. He knocked me into the table behind me, throwing the candles to the floor.

I looked back at him, ignoring the flames that were now on the ground licking to find more to burn. I leapt at Jedhail, managing to knock him backwards but he moved to punch me and I ducked. I crouched and spun trying to knock him off his feet but he jumped back avoiding the fall. We were both oblivious to the flames now eating into the structure of the church.

He spun and kicked me in the chest, throwing me into the wall. I crashed hard to the floor and fell unconscious for a moment. In my comatose state, I saw Rhys screaming my name. I woke to find the building falling victim to the flames and Jedhail was gone.

The jerk! He had the perfect moment to kill me and he didn't. I pushed myself up from the ground and walked out of the church. Then I saw Jedhail in the distance; he smiled at me before disappearing into the darkness. I stood in the pouring rain, the memory of thirty-five years ago echoing in my mind.

It took a moment for my anger to resurface. I ran from the church into the darkness Jedhail had disappeared into. I climbed the fence and steadied myself in a tree. I could sense him, he was not far off. Jumping onto the nearest roof, I began to run over rooftops, as a bolt of lightning flashed within the sky and I lost my footing and fell. My arm slammed into the roof's tiles before I rolled off on to the ground below. I coughed up mud I swallowed from landing face first. As my breathing returned to normal, I pushed myself off the ground and used the house to support myself. I sighed, Jedhail was long gone.

I felt as though this was just a game to him, like he didn't want to kill me. But why?

I killed her.

I was done. I couldn't do this anymore. I was out. He won.

I struggled back to my house, a beautiful stone mansion with large windows, draped in blood red curtains to hide our secrets within the house. I wandered up to my room and began packing my things to send them to my parents' address. Next, I wrote a fire letter to send directly to them saying I was coming home. I looked at the moonless sky; there were only a few hours of night left. I went into my brother's room and lay on his bed, falling asleep imagining that Rhys was there holding me.

I would no longer pursue my vendetta. Tomorrow I would return to my family, refusing to waste my immortal life hunting someone who wouldn't kill me when he had the chance.

# CHAPTER FOUR

As I walked away from the home I grew up in, it did something to my soul. This was where all my memories lived. I locked the front door and walked away without a glance back. I'd sent everything ahead to my parents' house, so I carried only a duffle bag, containing clothes and weapons, which I threw over my shoulder. I snuck a peek back as I continued walking away but didn't turn.

I put my headphones in, and listened to music as I walked out of Versattali. My hair blew gently in the breeze. I reached for the locket around my neck, closing my eyes as I held it to my chest – it was a small, flat, silver pendant with a heart and double infinity symbol carved into it. On the back was A + R. For Arya and Rhys. I opened my eyes and caught a quick glance at the small tattoo on my wrist – a black cat.

A small part of me felt a pull to walk through Vila, but fear and darkness also arose at the thought of standing within the destruction. So I walked straight ahead, and crossed over the border into Krypto. It had been thirty-five years since I had seen or spoken to my family. I was filled with guilt and regret over it, but I never knew what to say to them. I'd received letters from them, but I'd never responded – the letters were always the same:

*Arya,*

*Please come home. I know you're hurting, we all are. You're not the only one who lost him. Let go of this foolish revenge, we can still be a family. Just because you lost him, doesn't mean you are alone.*

*Let us know you are safe. We miss you.*
*Much love – Mum, Dad, Raiyn and Lorelei.*

It was a long walk to Skarsgard – a long path with the mountains so close. I hoped I didn't have to cross paths that would make me stray to the magic realm.

Azriel was made up of five magic kingdoms, nineteen mortal towns, and a town that sat on both – there were also the unclaimed lands, but no one dared to go there.

Why did my family choose to move to Skarsgard? If I were to make a guess, I would say because it was one of the furthest towns away from Versattali. They moved a month after Rhys was killed. But I stayed behind to claim my revenge.

How was I going to tell them I failed? I wasted all those years for nothing, and didn't get my revenge. He had won and no matter what I did, I couldn't erase the sight of blood from my hand. I couldn't even understand why I wanted the revenge so bad. It wasn't like it would bring them back.

In the distance, I saw nightfall begin to cover the skies. I checked into Krypto Hills Motel under the name Lucy Smith; I didn't want to risk Jedhail following me. As I sat in the restaurant alone, eating my meal, I wondered how my family would react at my return. I imagined Mum and Raiyn to be overjoyed, Lorelei would be pissed, but I had no idea how Dad would react. I suddenly got the feeling someone was watching me. Looking up, I scanned the tables filled with couples engrossed in conversation and lust. I turned around and saw a man sitting alone at the bar with a grey hood on, but he seemed too lost in his book to be watching me. I heard the empty chair at my table get pulled back. Looking across the table I saw a young blonde man in a suit sitting before me.

'Could I join you for a drink?' he asked in a very proper voice as the waitress cleared my plate.

I smiled from the corner of my mouth. 'If you're buying.'

He smirked and signalled the waiter who brought over a bottle of red wine and two glasses. The man in the suit poured, handing me a glass.

I bit my lip as I picked up the glass. 'I'm Lucy,' I purred. 'And you are?'

'Daniel Woodsen,' he said after taking a sip of his wine.

As we drank our way through the bottle of wine I laughed at his jokes and made small talk, careful not to reveal any large important details about me. As I finished my last glass he signalled for the cheque.

'May you accompany me for a walk?' he asked, his hand held out towards me.

I smiled as I took his hand and stood from my seat. He didn't release my hand as we walked through the corridors. He stopped at a door and looked deep into my eyes. I licked my lips and smiled at him as he bent down and kissed me, his hand wrapping around me pulling me closer to him. He unlocked the door and we entered his room. I pushed him onto the bed and kissed him deeply, craving to feel something. He rolled over and entrapped me beneath him, he leant down and kissed me again, then down my neck. *Feel something, dammit!* His lips returned to mine and I started to unbutton his top. That's when I noticed the tattoo on his collarbone: a deer skull with an arrow through its eyes. That was the symbol of the Wyatt Hunters. I pushed Daniel off me and jumped off the bed.

'I have to go to the bathroom,' I said, as he looked at me confused. 'Have to pee so badly. All that wine. I'll be quick. Sorry.'

Quickly, I turned and ran into the bathroom, locking the door behind me. Glancing around the room I wondered how I was going to get out of this. Did he know I wasn't human? Was I in a trap?

The window! Genius! I rushed to it, and pulled it open as quietly as I possibly could, climbing out of it with great difficulty, crashing into the bush on the other side of the window.

Not wasting a second, I ran back to my own room, locking the door behind me and closed the curtains.

The next day I continued my walk to Starlex. On the horizon, I could see the mountains that separated us from the magic realm, an ache inside my heart burned as I wished to cross those mountains. My one true anchor to this world lay on the other side of those mountains. If you looked closely into the mortal realm you would find a lot of us magical creatures hiding and living as humans – some out of shame, some because they wanted to be normal, some because they simply didn't fit in or mostly because they didn't agree with the supernatural politics.

I found a small motel in Starlex called Starlight, which I checked into. I still had the feeling of being watched so I hid in my room and lay on the bed, staring at the ceiling. I suddenly remembered I knew someone in the next town. I sat and looked over at the night stand where I saw a phone book. I got up, and grabbed it. Flicking through the pages until I found the name *Atlanta, Aurora*.

I picked up the room phone and dialled the number in the book, pacing back and forth, as far as the phone cord allowed me to, whilst I waited for an answer.

'Hello?' said a voice, finally.

'May I speak to Aurora please?' I asked politely.

'This is she.'

I sighed. 'It's Arya, could I crash at yours for a few nights?'

She paused. I was worried she would ask questions.

'You're finally going home,' she said. I could tell she was smiling. 'You're welcome to stay.'

'Thank you,' I said, releasing the breath I didn't realise I had been holding. 'I'll be there sometime tomorrow evening.'

As I hung up I wondered how long fear would keep me holed up at her place. Surely if I stayed a week she would start encouraging me to continue my way. I lay back on the bed and closed my eyes, falling into a deep sleep and into a dream I'd had for the past few nights. I was standing on top of a waterfall looking down into the rock pools where a girl in a black dress stood staring at her reflection, though she was confused because her reflection was wearing a white dress. In the trees watching her I saw Jareth, my old flame and now enemy. I watched the girl fall beneath the water and felt my lungs fill with water. I woke up gasping for air.

I wondered if my pit-stop to Aurora's house would be more trouble than just going to another hotel. It was barely dawn but I was wide awake, so I got up and started to pack. I checked out and walked to a bus stop that went to the border of Mystique, the temptation to cross the mountains testing my self-control. So I just focused on my book.

The bus ride was quiet, especially since I was the only one on the bus. It was nightfall when I got off. I walked through the quiet town and wondered if I could be happy in this life, the life my family had chosen. I turned around suddenly, sensing Jareth's presence, but what would he be doing here?

In the distance, I heard music, if you could call whatever they were playing that. I followed the sound until I reached a street that was all deserted, but for the building at the end. I walked into one of the empty houses to hide my bag before I went towards the music. It was an abandoned church. I saw the girl from my dreams standing on the steps, looking around as though she could sense me watching her.

Jareth's presence was stronger here, so I entered the church, the music blasting my ears. I followed the girl from my dreams to the bar and watched her and her friends have blue shots. I hoped it wasn't what I thought it was. I ordered myself a water but kept my eyes on her. She had Cassandra's blue eyes and beautiful curls.

I watched her walk outside and stalked her through the crowd. That's when I saw him. As the girl sat on the church steps Jareth approached her. I watched, waiting for him to strike but he didn't do anything. I hid out of view as he brought her back into the church and onto the dancefloor. I drank my glass of water and pulled out a small knife. I cut deep into my wrist and let the cup fill with blood. As Jareth left her alone on the dancefloor I ran up to her, I pulled her head back and forced my blood down her throat before disappearing into the crowd.

I ran back to the house where I had hidden my bag My wrist was already healed, only a red stain remained. I sat in the window of the house waiting for her to walk past. If he did try and hurt her at least she now had my blood in her system.

# CHAPTER FIVE

The next morning, I decided to stay in the house in the deserted street. I could still feel Jareth's presence in the town and I didn't want him sensing mine. Two days later I finally left and went to Aurora's home. The moment I saw her house a calmness washed over me.

I had barely knocked once when Aurora's friendly, familiar face met me at the door We hadn't seen each other for seventeen years but we had always been close. She hadn't aged a day, but I noticed she now wore more motherly clothes, probably to keep up appearances. Her green eyes were full of warmth as she ushered me inside.

Aurora was a witch, as was her sister Cassandra, to whom I owe my existence, just as much as my parents, perhaps even more.

'It's so amazing to see you,' Aurora said as she embraced me.

I followed her up to the guest room, sensing her pain of being so close to Alesmera and not being able to enter it. Her resistance must have been strong to stay away for sixteen years without any news or contact from the other side.

'What's wrong with you?' she asked as I threw my bag on the bed. I looked at her, confused. 'I may have made my powers dormant but my ability to read auras has remained.'

'What do you see?' I asked, not meeting her eyes.

'You used to be bright colours, now you're dark,' she whispered. 'I didn't think your mother's kind could project these colours.'

I met her eyes. 'I'm working on it – I just…I need…'

'I know,' she said before I could finish my sentence, understanding my unspoken words.

She left the room and I heard the stairs creak as she walked downstairs. I undressed and wrapped the towel she left on the bed around me. I tried the shower in the room but the hot water wasn't working. I crossed the hall and entered what looked like a teenager's room with lots of purple, purple bedsheets, curtains, walls, everything was purple. *Very unnerving*. I walked into the bathroom and sighed in relief to find the hot water worked. I stepped into the shower, the warmth caressed my skin.

From downstairs, I heard arguing. It was faint but I picked up the words, 'Heir of Aubrey'. I turned off the water. As I wrapped the towel around me I heard the door of the room I was in slam shut.

'He is still alive you know,' I said as I walked out from the bathroom in just my towel.

The girl looked at me in shock, not from who I was but what I said intrigued her more.

'I'm Arya. The guest bathroom doesn't have hot water.'

'You look familiar,' she questioned.

'I should, I saved your life.'

She answered me with a blank look. I rolled my eyes. 'I poured the blood down your throat at that hormonal dance you attended.'

I could sense the darkness in her. The question was, was she more her father or her mother. I left the room, leaving her unsatisfied with our conversation.

***

The next morning, I lay in bed until I heard the house empty, leaving only Aurora and myself. I joined her downstairs on the couch where I found her with her nose in a book.

'Why did you finally choose to return to your family?' Aurora asked, as she put the book down.

I looked into her deep green eyes.

'I was so set on revenge,' I whispered. 'I forgot about those who still live.'

'Have you been home lately?'

I looked away from her. I knew she meant Illyragasia – the magic world I am meant to rule.

I shook my head. 'The Ecuador still have their political ruling system, like they have since...'

'Your mother was denied the throne,' Aurora finished.

I nodded.

The Ecuadorian System was made up of Nagual, Witches and Vampires. They'd always had their own private system but since my mother was dethroned and I declined my ascension they took charge and had stayed in power.

'Most of my mother's kin now hide in the mountains. Some still live in Alesmera but most fled after Cassandra's...'

I couldn't finish the sentence.

# CHAPTER SIX

The stars glistened in the night sky as I sat at the window in the lounge room. A book lay open in my hand but I couldn't bring my mind around to read the words. I gazed blankly at the pages, the lines blurred before my eyes.

Hearing the front door open, I suddenly felt that connection that vibrated between Ariella and I. A blood connection. Cassandra always said this could occur but I'd never heard of one happening. I felt fear coming from Ariella.

'You're troubled,' I said, not looking up to meet her gaze. 'I can sense it. You need to learn to hide your emotions.'

Ariella walked into the lounge room and stood before me, asking how she could learn to do such a thing.

'Self-control,' I muttered without looking at her. 'It won't work, your plan, mortals know nothing of our world.'

She sat before me, and tried convincing herself as much as me that her plan would work. I looked up from my book. She was stronger than she knew; if she got the right training.

'Perhaps,' I said, holding the book to my chest. 'But just because your friend can search information on the internet, it doesn't make her an expert. She doesn't know anything about magic and she won't be able to find the magical protections that are around that house, but you can. You'll be able to feel the magic's imprint. It'll take you a while to learn how to read the imprints, but if you sense it, find a different way.'

I held my hand out to her before she could say another word. She hesitantly took my hand. I felt a rush of power crossed between us from the connection as I whispered an incantation in my mind. Above us the thunder began to crash, and the rain prepared to fall.

She snatched her hand away and I laughed under my breath. That touch of power was enough to make me go back to my addiction. The thing people don't tell you about magic, is that it's like a drug, and when you're addicted to something and your emotions rule you, that's when you lose control.

'Better sneak up to your room. Aurora just woke up, and Ariella, my bet's on the number three,' I whispered, then turned back to my book. Three of her friends were loyal to her, the others would betray her.

I didn't sleep that night. I was sitting at the table with a green tea early that morning when Aurora came downstairs and asked me what was wrong. I wanted, and needed to tell someone about Vila. Would she look at me differently? Would she judge me?

'What do they say happened to Vila?' I asked.

Aurora looked at me, puzzled. 'That a fire got out of control and killed all the residents. No one got out. Why do you ask?'

'It was me,' I said softly, not meeting her eyes.

'What do you mean it was you?' Aurora asked.

'I dabbled in dark magic and it consumed me,' I explained, my voice soft, remembering that empty feeling. 'Whilst under the black influence I went to Vila and destroyed it in my rage.'

Aurora came and kneeled before me. She ran her fingers through my hair. 'That's why you ran?' she questioned.

I nodded.

'You have a good heart and soul,' Aurora whispered. 'Remember I can see your aura.'

I smiled at her, but then a weird look crossed her face. She walked back to her seat and looked over at me.

'You could kill him. Ariella wouldn't have to be compromised,' Aurora said hopefully.

'I can't,' I replied, frowning at her. 'I could never kill Jareth.'

'What do you mean you can't? I thought you were strong enough?'

'Against Jareth?' I scoffed. 'I could kill that spoilt brat in a heartbeat, but I won't.'

*Because I loved him once.*

'But Ariella will die if she faces him. You must kill him'

'I can't,' I snapped, standing up. 'If I killed him it would bring around another supernatural war. We are still trying to recover from the last one. Do you remember that? Do you really want to relive it?'

Aurora sagged down into the chair. I went over and kneeled before her, taking her hand in mine as I met her eyes.

'Ariella is strong and since we have a blood connection, I will keep it open and not let her die. I promise,' I whispered.

I dismissed myself from the table to go for a walk. Wandered past Jareth's mortal home. Even here he over compensated. I walked through to the forest to where I saw a blue light outlining a door; the doorway through the mountains.

'Do you dare enter?' said a dark voice I knew too well.

I looked to my side to see a hologram of Aubrey, the king of Alesmera. He was worlds away, but he could still astral project himself back as he pleased to check in on his kingdom without anyone's knowledge.

'What is it you wish, my Lord?' I enquired.

'Why is it that you help my daughter ascend to the throne? Are you trying to unite the five kingdoms like the prophecy requires?'

'Never,' I snapped. 'I will not allow the Battles for Azriel to take place. I will not risk the rise of purgatory.'

'Then why do you assist my daughter?' he asked, standing before me. Even as a hologram I could feel his power.

'I don't assist her to the throne, only on the path her mother followed,' I said. 'Besides, Adestria is too busy fighting for Daddy's attention to realise Mycenae is hers, Illyria knows nothing of her immortal heritage and lastly, Ekaterina refuses to acknowledge her powers.'

Aubrey smiled at me as though he knew something I did not.

'As you say, Your Highness,' he said before disappearing.

# CHAPTER SEVEN

The next day Ariella burst into my room demanding I lead her and her friends into Alesmera, which I agreed to with a motivation of my own; I needed to contact the gatekeeper.

As we stood at the edge of Jareth's property looking into the forest that held the doorway, I felt the power the land held. This was the easiest way into the magic realm. You could climb the mountains which would take days but Styr's realm was quicker and simpler. I counted Jareth's guards. Only four. He mustn't have known I was in town; his father must have kept that quiet. I pulled out a pen and paper and wrote, *Druids have been roaming the mountain sides, is this Jareth's doing? I've also felt as though someone is watching me, but it's not Jedhail – any idea who?*

I handed the note to Ariella and told her to give it to Styr, then winked at her before I walked over to the guards and had them unconscious in less than a minute.

'Jareth is in Alesmera,' I said as the last guard fell unconscious.

'What is a blood connection?' I heard Ariella yell as I walked away but I ignored her and kept walking.

It was time for me to leave Mystique. I had a fleeting goodbye with Aurora. She was still worried but I assured her all was fine.

'What if Ariella gets in trouble?' she argued.

'I couldn't go in with her, I'm sorry. For one Jareth would cause a war if he thought I was too involved just to prove his power, and secondly, Grandfather would have words to say.'

'You talk to your grandparents?'

'We ended on bad terms, but all will be forgotten if I agree to follow the path he sets for me.'

Hugging her goodbye, I turned on my heels and walked away. It was time for me to head home.

I crossed through Robin Falls to Skarsgard. Woodlands surrounded a lot of the area. It was cute but just another small town I guess.

As I was walking, a fireball appeared before me and landed in my hand. The flame dispersed revealing a piece of paper. It was Styr's reply: *He searches for Elphina's bones, did you hide them well? Druids have dark magics that could use many spells with her bones. With your follower I am not sure, but he is not supernatural. Be safe my highness.*

I walked through town until I was standing before my parents' relocated home. They had set up a human life, a simple double story brick house, two door garage and a mailbox on a fresh, green lawn. The sight made me want to roll my eyes. As I walked towards the door my stomach filled with butterflies. What if they were mad at me? What if they didn't want to see me?

As my mind filled with "what ifs" my older sister Lorelei stepped out the front door. Her silky bronze hair fell to her elbows and her almond skin glistened in the sunlight. Lorelei and I were never actually close. I always felt like she disliked me. The wind blew her hair around her face, as her golden eyes met mine and a sweet fragrance hit my nose. I was sure it was a candy perfume. Horrid stuff.

'Well,' she scoffed. 'If it isn't the great Arya Faith,' she said with cold sarcasm.

'Misplaced the De-Valentino didn't you, Sis?' I snarled back just as coldly. I felt anger swell inside me, my cat-like teeth appearing.

'You don't deserve that name,' she spat.

'Still, I'm the only child with the pure De-Valentino blood; now where is Nefertiti?'

Lorelei hissed at these last words, showing her teeth. When I didn't back down she growled, and called for my mother Nefertiti before walking away from the house. Lorelei was angry at me for abandoning them all those years ago, but she was also angry at me returning. I closed my eyes and calmed my emotions, my teeth returning to normal.

Remembering back to when I was a child, Lorelei and I had always had a bad relationship. When I was maybe seven, I remembered watching her for hours as she sat before her mirror applying make-up to make herself more beautiful. I used to beg her to teach me but even back then she didn't want anything to do with me.

Nefertiti came to the door and a large lump suddenly appeared in my throat.

'Hey Mum,' I whispered.

I held my breath waiting for a reaction like Lorelei's; instead tears welled up in her eyes and she pulled me into a hug. I held onto her as though scared to let her go again. When she released me, I looked her over. Her coffee brown hair shone in the sunlight against her tanned olive skin, her dark brown eyes held a kindness that I had forgotten. A wave of guilt and regret washed over me. I had kept her in the dark for all these years, and here I was now, just moving back in under her roof.

'What'd you do with the house?' she asked as she led me up the stairs to my new bedroom.

'I didn't do anything. I kept it in good order and locked it up before I left,' I said softly.

'We wrote,' she said, not looking at me.

'I know,' I said guilty. 'I don't have a good excuse to why I didn't reply. I'm sorry.'

She opened the door at the end of the hall. 'I hope this is fine. I'll let you unpack,' she said with another smile and hug before she turned and walked back downstairs. I watched her go, knowing I should call out to her and say something, but I couldn't. I had too much to say but nothing came to mind. I unpacked all my things and then sat on the bed. I looked around the room and couldn't help but feel a little claustrophobic, but I wasn't sure why. The room was spacious; I had a queen size bed against the wall in the corner plus a bathroom and a walk-in wardrobe.

I walked over to the window and watched as the colours of the sunset bled into each other. It's the first time I had been in a quiet life. I felt motionless from the lack of adrenaline and the alienation from my vendetta tore at my soul. My thoughts were screaming murder but my lips remained silent, fighting the battle that seemed to haunt my mind.

I went back to bed and attempted to turn my racing mind off by listening to the ticking of the clock, but sleep was still evading me. I turned my gaze to the open window again. The air and moonlight were so calm, the night silent. Hours later I finally fell into an uneasy sleep. A soft voice echoed in my mind. Without waking up I searched for a presence around me but I was alone. I must be in a dream. I listened to the voice:

*'And as the moon and sun lay down their weapons, she felt at peace, human again, a feeling that was long ago stolen from her...'*

'That's beautiful,' I said, connecting to the words. 'Did you write it?'

The voice didn't continue, but why would me speaking stop the passage, this was a dream.

'What are you?' the voice said. 'How are you speaking to me?'

I stayed silent, this was a dream, wasn't it? No one could speak to me though a dream, could they? But I checked, there was no presence nearby. Intrigued, I found myself wanting to know more, to hear his voice again.

'I'm nothing but ordinary, it was you that entered my mind.'

He didn't say anything back so I closed my mind fully and finally fell into a deep sleep, where my deepest, darkest fears and desires hid. My dreams started off in the deepest corner of my mind. I saw Mikhail standing beneath a tree ahead of me. I ran over to him and threw my arms around him, pulling him in for a kiss. His arms wrapped around me as though he never wanted to let me go. We walked down into the forest and lay beside the lake where I curled up against his chest and closed my eyes.

I opened my eyes to find myself lying on the grass alone.

'Mum isn't going to be happy that you're lying in wet grass,' said a voice I knew all too well. I looked up as Rhys walked over and lay beside me. He tucked my hair behind my ear. 'We both can show up at the party with dirty clothes,' he whispered, and kissed my cheek.

I blinked and found myself standing in Rhys's bedroom, Jedhail stood behind Rhys. He smiled at me as he snapped his neck, I screamed as I watched my worst nightmare happen again before my eyes. I could never stop it. Jedhail's laugh echoed in my mind.

# CHAPTER EIGHT

I woke quickly, the images in my dreams ending with a sudden jolt. I looked at the time; it was 8.05am. I had less than an hour till school. I sat on my bed staring at my blank wall wondering what I'd gotten myself into. I didn't go to school, I didn't need to, and I didn't want to meet and get attached to mortals. I got up and walked to my mirror, my eyes trailed down my hour glass body. I sighed, as weird as it sounds I wish I could look at my reflection and find flaws — I know that sounds a little vain but my mother's genes were definitely passed onto me. I didn't like being desired, it attracted all the crazies.

I walked down the stairs to find an empty house. I sat at the round, wooden table in the centre of the kitchen, surrounded by dark panelled walls and white tiled floors. It was a nice house, sure, but it wasn't home; it didn't feel like a safe place for me to run back to.

I missed home. I closed my eyes remembering back to the elegant parties we used to throw.

I remembered wearing a silk dress with beads for straps, multiple strands of pearls and diamonds hung around my neck, heels that would glisten in the light, gloves that ran up my arms. As I entered the door, the scent of mystic essence and sweet seduction would promise to take away the worries of the next morning. In the corner would be a piano and a man in a suit singing songs about love and freedom. The bartender would greet me with a smile as he handed me my drink. That's where I'd spend most of the night, people watching.

I blinked away the memories, reminding myself that this was now, that was the past. I got up and walked back upstairs to my room. I noticed photos on the wall as I walked up the stairs. They hadn't taken any photos since I had left. I turned away from the photos, and ran upstairs to my room.

Since it was storming outside I pulled on jeans and a sweater, hoping it would help me blend in. I'd never been to a mortal school before, so I didn't even know what to pack really. I threw a note pad and some pens into a bag hoping that was all that I would need. I walked out of my room, avoiding looking in the mirror again. I was always scared of my black eyes coming back.

I stood in our doorway looking out into the street slick with rain, wondering if high school kids would judge me for showing up at school drenched. I didn't know where my parents kept the umbrellas in our house. I sucked it up and stepped out into the rain. Luckily the school was only four streets away.

New town, new school. Oh god, I was going to be the shiny new toy. Kill me now. As I walked towards the administration building the wind circled around me and the scent of blood hit my nose. I looked towards the forest. It was probably just animals fighting or a dead crow. I looked back at the administration building again before I started walking towards the forest.

Watching my step once I was in the trees, I stayed as silent as possible. I could hear footsteps up ahead - human footsteps - but there wasn't a human scent in here. I walked further into the trees and had to slap my hand to my mouth to stop a gasp. Three foxes lay dead in the clearing. I stepped closer, kneeling over them. They'd been drained of blood.

A twig snapped somewhere ahead of me. I quickly ran back to the school, reaching the administration building just in time to hear the bell ring.

Instead of participating in first period, I was stuck in the administration's office signing forms, organising classes, and getting a rule list. If I'd known it was going to be this much work I may not have signed up. I wondered why my parents decided that my siblings needed to start doing this. The bell for the break rang and I was still filling out forms. Why were there so many pages?

Was it necessary to know every little detail about me? Did I have to write that I was female? Can you not just pick up on that when I come into the office? If you were a spy and ever needed to learn about someone you could just steal their school files; it had every single detail. What religion was I? Wiccan?

Students walked in and out of the office during the break and each time someone walked past where I sat, I could feel their eyes on me. The bell rang for end of break just as I finished the forms. I left the office and walked to second period, which per my timetable was Modern History. Ha! I could just tell them my life, that was modern history, right?

As I turned the corner without looking, someone bumped into me and I dropped all my sheets and books I'd just collected. Honestly, since I wasn't looking, it was probably me that ran into them but that was not the point. I knelt to pick them all up, resisting an eye roll. Someone knelt before me holding out a pen of mine that had rolled away. I looked up and felt my breath catch. His storm grey eyes had a mesmerising glow to them.

'You dropped this,' he said, in a deep voice.

I snatched my pen from him, standing up and walking away. What was that? He wasn't human, right? There was no way a human could make my heart race like that.

As I sat in Modern History I zoned out, especially since half the stories the teacher discussed I wanted to rewrite because the mortals missed large, significant details about the wars.

'I'm Matt,' said the guy beside me, breaking my daydream about rainbows and lollypops or something or other.

I smiled innocently at his ocean blue eyes, looking over his black-only attire. If he didn't smell human I'd think he was a vampire with his pale skin and ebony hair.

'Are you nervous about starting mid-semester?' he asked.

'Of course she isn't,' interrupted the tanned, blonde, body-builder beside him. 'She was probably prom queen and the most popular girl in her old school. She has it wrapped.' He turned to me. 'I'm Logan, by the way.'

I took in his mocha eyes. 'Arya, and actually I was home-schooled,' I said, with a small, teasing smile at both of them.

'Wow!' Logan exclaimed. 'Are you kidding? That doesn't happen around here. Why were you home-schooled?'

Mum told me that if someone asked this, lie. Tell them it was because we moved around a lot, it was easier to home-school us rather than put us in and out of schools. But truth is, my parents didn't want to risk me accidently using magic in front of the mortal kids. Then, as I grew up, I lost interest in wanting to check out mortal schools. I had my supernatural friends and teachers who I respected and who could teach me things I actually wanted to learn.

'What class do you have next?' Matthew asked.

I pulled out my schedule, *MATHS*. I showed him my schedule which got him excited.

'Looks like we are in the same class for Maths as well.'

I smiled at him. At least I'd have someone to show me where the classroom was.

When the bell for lunch rang, Matthew threw his arm around my shoulders and walked me to the cafeteria. I mentally sighed in relief when I saw that he and Logan sat with girls as well.

'I had my meeting with the guidance councillor this morning, you know, the meeting about my future. I told her I want to go to the mountains,' Matthew was telling us. 'I want to be an archaeologist; how brilliant will that be?!'

'You want to study rocks?' Logan sneered. 'I am going to be a lawyer, I will totally rule the courtrooms.'

Matthew threw a chip from his lunch at Logan, 'You're such a dick, do you even know what an archaeologist is?'

Logan shrugged and ate the chip Matthew threw at him and smirked.

Kirstin, one of the girls at the table, excused herself to go to the bathroom. I asked to go with her to find out where they were. As we walked out of the hall I wondered if she and Matthew were a thing. They both had that vampire look down. Kirstin was almost unhealthy thin with jet black hair with red highlights. She started telling me about how she was leaving at the end of the year to go study Human Behaviour and Law.

As we entered the bathroom I accidently ran into the girl leaving. A chill ran down my spine as my eyes took in her deep green eyes. A cold breeze was suddenly around me.

'Sorry,' the girl said before stepping around me. I looked back at her; her short, black hair brushed against her shoulders and her skin had a rosiness to it that made me feel like she had just fed.

'Don't bother,' said Kirstin as she continued into the bathroom. 'I'm surprised you even got a sorry. They don't talk to anyone outside of their group.'

I waited outside the bathroom for Kirstin. Another cold chill ran down my spine. I turned to see a girl who looked like she belonged in a swimwear magazine walk past, her blonde hair bouncing with each step.

Kirstin walked out of the bathroom and we made our way back to the cafeteria, I asked her what the other girl at our tables' name was.

'Do you mean the blonde girl in the pink?' Kirstin asked. I nodded. She must wear pink a lot if that's how she was described. 'Yeah that's Missy. There is another girl in our group too. She should be there by the time we get back.'

We sat back down at the table and I noticed Missy staring off into the distance. Her hair had thousands of layers, that were pointing in all different directions. Kirstin sat beside her and stole a chocolate out of her lunch box. Missy didn't even notice. She was too focused on whatever she was looking at.

'Logan?' she said in a dazed voice. 'Do you think I'm pretty?'

Logan looked in the direction she was looking before answering her. 'I think you are the most beautiful girl in the room so forget about the stiff. He's an idiot for not noticing you.'

I now looked in the direction she was staring, and saw the two girls I had seen earlier. They sat at a table with a guy who was busy reading. It was the guy I had run into in the hallway - I wasn't forgetting those storm-like eyes anytime soon.

'Who are they?' I asked Missy.

She looked at me for a second before focusing her eyes back on him. 'The girls are Raven and Echo, I don't really know much about them. But him?' she said with a small sigh. 'That is Christopher Jackson, and he's never even bothered to look in my direction.'

I didn't know if I should laugh or feel sorry for Missy and her crush on Christopher Jackson. Though, I understood where the crush came from. Those eyes could make any girl weak at the knees. He definitely wasn't human.

I looked at the table next to Christopher's and saw a face that made me smile. I excused myself to Missy and walked across the cafeteria. As I walked past Christopher our eyes met and I felt a cold fire run through my chest.

I reached Raiyn's table and whispered, 'Hey.'

Raiyn got out of his chair and embraced me. I looked over his shoulder at Lorelei who looked annoyed at me for interrupting their conversation. She ignored the fact I was there and kept talking to the other students at the table.

'I couldn't believe it when Mum told me you were home. You were asleep when I got in and I didn't want to wake you,' he said as he released me from the hug.

'Is it true you're here to stay?'

I laughed half-heartedly. 'I hope so, I missed you.'

He hugged me again and I had to blink away the tears. He looked so different. His messy black hair made his gold eyes stand out.

'What's with the underworld look?' I joked.

He winked at me. 'I'm being modern,' he teased. 'Have you seen Lorna yet?'

'Lorna?' I said with disbelief. 'As in my best friend Lorna? As in the girl that used to make Mikhail sleep on the floor?'

He nodded in a way that asked if there was another Lorna. I hugged him goodbye. I headed back to my table. I wanted to get my bag and then go find her.

As I went to pick up my bag, I noticed there was another girl at the table. My jaw dropped when I recognised her. She screamed and threw her arms around me.

'I can't believe you're here!' Lorna exclaimed. 'I didn't believe them when they said there was a girl in our group named Arya.'

Lorna Watson was a witch I had met back in 1915. We used to practise magic together when she wasn't with her coven. I regretted pushing her away after Mikhail died. Her dark brown curls flowed against her tanned skin, her brown eyes shone out and she still wore the sweet scent of roses that I remembered.

'How do you two know each other?' Matthew asked as we sat back down.

'We knew each other as children,' Lorna said.

The bell rang, ending our conversation. We had so much to catch up on. Though we couldn't say too much around the group.

I walked into Maths and cursed under my breath when I saw the only remaining seat was next to Christopher. I got a grip on myself, and walked to the back of the class, sitting down beside him. I pulled out my note book and pen.

The teacher walked in and called silence. I opened my note book, ready to start taking notes but instead I began sketching. I drew an archway. I recognised the arch I realised, it was in Alesmera. The blood connection, I realised, dropping the pen. Ariella was going well so far.

I turned to look at Christopher to find him staring at me. I looked away quickly, feeling him watching me. I looked back at him, holding his gaze this time. I really wanted to run my hands through that messy hair of his, and for him to hold me against his toned body and kiss me. The girl in front of me dropped her text book making me jump, I turned away from Christopher and collected my books, excusing myself from class.

# CHAPTER NINE

The flames of the fire burnt as high as they could reach in the fireplace, its bright light reflecting upon me. Even though I was looking into the flame, I could not see the fire. My mind was trapped a million miles away. Absentmindedly, my fingers traced the cat shaped birthmark on my wrist.

'What's on your mind?'

I looked up, as my father sat down on the couch beside me. I knew it isn't possible, but in the flames light he looked older, and more tired than he did last I saw him. Was it my fault? I wondered. His tanned skin looked darker in the dimmed light. His black hair was slicked back like it always was. I don't think I'd ever seen it messy.

'Nothing,' I said, shaking my head slightly.

'You know Arya,' he began to say, then paused for a minute. 'I'm glad you're home' he said, kissing my forehead.

I smiled, knowing that was not what he was planning on saying. His eyes looked down to my fingers tracing my tattoo.

'Not every Nagual is a black cat,' he said.

I looked at him and met his deep eyes.

'How is that even possible?' I asked.

'Well, very rarely, you'll come across a Nagual that takes the form of a bird, coyote, dog, or even a donkey - I've come across a coyote before, his tattoo was different to ours.'

I smiled, imagining someone walking around with a donkey tattoo on their wrist. I suppressed a laugh at the thought.

'Archer.'

We both looked up at the stairs. Nefertiti was standing on one of the higher steps. Archer smiled at his wife, then kissed me on the forehead before heading upstairs. I watched as the fire died away, my mind too awake to sleep just yet.

A slamming door broke my trance. I looked up, to see Lorelei running down the stairs and out into the night. I waited for Raiyn to run out after her but he didn't even open the door. After a moment, I got up and walked outside to find Lorelei sitting on the front of the driveway.

'Mind if I join you?' I asked as I reached her.

She shrugged, so I sat beside her.

'Are you okay?'

She ignored my question and asked one of her own. 'Why'd you come back?'

I had a sinking feeling that her and Raiyn's fight had been about me. I gave her a small smile and shrugged, looking up at the stars. At that moment, I wasn't sure why I had come back. I didn't feel welcomed back into the family. I felt like a stranger living in someone else's house.

'Why do you hate me so much?' I asked, turning to her. It was a question I had been asking her since I was a kid. She'd never answered me. She'd always ignored me and walked off.

'I don't hate you,' she snapped, surprising me. I caught her gaze and she sighed. 'You bring up old memories,' she said softly, looking out into the street.

'When I was human I was the first-born daughter. I was spoilt and had the perfect life. When I was seventeen my mum got pregnant again. It was a miracle. Even I was happy, I always wanted a younger sister. But when she was born, I became insignificant. So I ran away and almost got myself killed, but Archer found me, and I had parents again. I was the only daughter, and then you were born. And part of me felt insignificant again.'

I placed my hand on hers. 'You're not,' I whispered. 'Archer and Nefertiti love you. You're their favourite daughter.'

She pulled her hand away and gave me a weak smile. 'I'm sorry Arya, but can I just be alone for a while?'

'Lor – ' I began.

'Just go away, please,' she snapped, cutting me off.

I looked away from her and stood up. I started walking back inside when I paused and turned back to her.

'Do you miss them?' I asked.

'Who are you talking about?' she asked, turning to me.

'Your real parents.'

She hesitated for a moment as though she had never thought of this question, and then without meeting my eyes she said, 'No, there is nothing to miss.'

And without another word she turned away from me again. I knew she was lying but I didn't push it.

I wonder what it would be like to have another family. What was it like for Raiyn, Lorelei and … Rhys? Even though it was years ago, those people were her blood, her true relatives. How could she not miss them? Yes, they betrayed her but that didn't just erase the first seventeen years. I guessed I would never know. I was born, not made. I was lucky. I was a miracle.

When I got inside I walked up the stairs. I heard hushed whispering so I tiptoed over to my parents' room and put my ear to the door.

'What do you mean there's no need to panic? Veronica will never let it go, she's determined to put the curse in motion,' Nefertiti hissed.

'She will not fall for it; Arya is too strong' Archer replied calmly.

I wondered what they were talking about, but I heard my mother sigh which generally meant the end of a conversation. I walked to my room and fell onto my bed.

*When I fell asleep yellow eyes stared at me through the darkness. Eyes I had seen before, eyes of mischief and malice. A cold laugh echoed through the air, and then a whisper. 'The curse has already begun.'*

*Before me I saw my reflection, my eyes as black as night.*

# CHAPTER TEN

I woke up, throwing the sheets off me. My heart pounding against my chest and, even though the air had a cold bite to it, I was still sweating. Why were my dreams always so vivid? I turned to the clock on my bedside table; it was 8.40am. I had ten minutes to get ready for school. A few fire letters were scattered on my floor from Raiyn, all asking if I was coming to school today.

I made it to school looking flustered as though I had got out of bed and come straight in; which was what I had done but that was beside the point. I was late so I walked straight to class. As I entered the English room, Logan sat up and smiled at me, indicating he had saved a seat beside him. I smiled at him and went and sat down.

'You're late, Miss…?' the teacher enquired.

'De-Valentino, Sir. I'm sorry, it won't happen again.'

The teacher nodded and studied me over his half-moon glasses before turning to the blackboard, where he began writing something out of the text book.

As class progressed, I zoned out. I had never understood the concept of the subject. We all grew up learning to speak it, so was it right or proper to correct people on their way of speech? Like poetry, no one ever knows what they are going on about, and yet, we are forced to study them and learn to write them. What was the point?

'Language and emotion: putting words into feelings and feelings into words,' the teacher was saying.

Running my fingers back through my hair, I groaned. Emotions, really? We feel them constantly so why did we have to learn about them? Why was I even in school? This was pointless and a waste of time.

'Emotions come from our core and we use different emotions depending on the situation. There is anger, disgust, fear, happiness, sadness, love. We know the words but do we know the emotion?' the teacher continued. 'Miss DeValentino, can you explain the emotion love?'

Breaking from my daydream, I looked up at the teacher and he repeated his question, asking me what is love? Love? Out of all the emotions in the world this guy was asking me about love!

'Love...' I replied slowly, 'is friendship and passion?'

It was in that moment I heard the velvet voice within my mind. 'When was the last time you opened up to love?'

I closed my mind, offended at the question. He had no right to know or ask that. Though curiosity consumed me as to how he had asked.

I zoned back out as the teacher went on.

The bell for break finally rang. Logan and I walked to the cafeteria to meet the rest of the group. I didn't say much, too tired to join the conversation. Kristin and Logan were arguing about cars, Missy was staring at Christopher again, and Lorna was working on her homework for her next class which she hadn't completed the night before.

'Aw, I'm so jealous,' Missy suddenly said. I glanced up at her to find her looking at me. 'Christopher is staring at you.'

The whole table, except me, suddenly turned and looked at Christopher. I felt like face palming. Shrugging it off, I took a bite of the apple I'd had sitting in front of me. When the whole table had gone back to what they were doing I stole a glance at Christopher and found that he was indeed looking at me. I smiled slightly then looked away; I had a nagging feeling that I knew him from somewhere, but for the life of me I couldn't remember where.

It was raining as I made my way to Ancient History that afternoon. I pulled my hood up to protect myself from the rain. Once inside the classroom I saw that my desk was still free. I sighed out of relief as I sat down, taking my note pad out and sketching again, hoping my mind would again subconsciously let me know that Ariella was fine. I heard the seat beside me move but I didn't look up.

'Do you draw often?' he asked, moving his chair slightly closer.

I looked over into Christopher's eyes, grey as slate. 'When I'm not focusing on class,' I teased.

'It's beautiful,' he said, looking down at the page. I smiled, turning to look up at the teacher to distract myself from wanting to stare at his lips.

'What's your story then?'

I looked at him questioningly. I paused, giving myself more time to think of something. I didn't think he'd want to hear about the death and wars that I'd lived through. 'I lived in Versattali with my family.'

'But they have been here for years, right? You only just got here.'

I forced a smile. 'I didn't want to leave my home, and there was unfinished business I had in town.' Business which every inch in my body desired to finish. The magic swirled in me, craving for release. I was like a tiger in a small cage and I wanted to escape.

'I'm guessing it's finished now then,' he said.

*I wish,* I thought silently to myself. I tried to imagine what it would be like if it was over. I looked over at him, my eyes travelling to his lips. I saw his eyes travel to my lips too and I knew he was thinking the same thing as I was.

I jumped, feeling my heart racing in fear. I turned away from Christopher. *Stupid,* I thought to myself. He was mortal. His life would be over in a few short years. Then I realised this fear wasn't mine.

I looked down at what I had sketched and was surprised to see a sketch of a guy. He looked like Tatiana's son. It could be him; he'd be that age by now. He was on our side as far as I knew so Ariella should be fine. Her fear would pass.

# CHAPTER ELEVEN

Have you ever watched a sunset? The way the colours bled into each other was a different kind of beautiful. I stood at my window watching the darkness claim the sky, begging my mind to let go of the kaleidoscopic memories that haunted my thoughts. Had I not endured enough pain to last multiple lifetimes? My blue eyes reflected out at me. I remembered how Aurora said my aura had darkened. How had I become this?

The house was silent. Everyone was either in their rooms or out. I was so tired that I wished I could sleep. It was something peaceful, something I could never experience. I opened my hand before me and let a small white flame spark. I let it rise higher, controlling the level of the magic. Slowly, I put my hands together, letting the flame die, wondering how long it'd take me to use any magic again properly without consequence and fear.

I crawled into bed and watched the shadows crawl over me, listening to the clock tick later into the night. I finally fell asleep. The dream I had was so real that I could feel the cold air against my skin in the garden that I stood in. I looked down and found myself in a gold and black ball gown. Brushing my hair back, I found a mask on my face. Looking around, I saw an archway and I walked towards it, picking up a lantern that sat beside me, and exited the garden. From behind me someone took hold of my hand. I turned to see a masked figure in a suit.

He pressed his lips to my hand. I smiled and put the lantern back on the ground.

He pulled me towards him and danced us into a slow circle as I bit my lip in nervousness. He leaned in and kissed me, moving me back until I felt the garden wall hit my back. The kiss continued. The night air felt cooler, or perhaps I was just falling deeper into the dream. His lips moved to my neck and I was suddenly overwhelmed with fear, a fear I hadn't felt in years, but it was too late, his teeth had broken my skin.

I woke screaming. My bedroom door burst open and Raiyn ran to my side. I curled up in his arms.

'It was just a dream,' he whispered reassuringly, whilst I caught my breath. He stroked my hair, helping me calm myself. It had all felt so real. I knew I had intense dreams but this was a whole new level. I lay back down and Raiyn curled under the blanket, wrapping his arms around me. He kissed my cheek and soon fell asleep beside me.

With him there, I fell into a dreamless sleep.

The next morning, I woke up in bed by myself. Raiyn had probably gotten up and gone back to his room during the night. I was still grateful to him for staying with me till I was asleep. I got out of bed and went to the bathroom to tie my hair up in a ponytail when I noticed fang marks and dry blood on my neck. It couldn't have been from the dream, could it? That was just great! Now my dreams were slowly killing me. I washed my neck then I let my hair fall back down, tying a scarf around my neck.

This was just freaking typical. I leave my vendetta to avoid a vampire and now one haunts my dreams. I bet Jedhail was somehow behind this.

I walked to school and went straight to first period, stopping to talk to no one. I couldn't concentrate on the class, my mind continually replaying the dream. Perhaps I had just imagined the bite marks this morning and when I got home they wouldn't be there anymore. I hoped. I adjusted the scarf as the bell rang but it was a lost cause. Someone was going to notice eventually. Most likely Raiyn when I got home.

I went and sat next to Matthew when I got to the cafeteria. I noticed he was wearing a band t-shirt today, like he had every day now that I think about it.

'What is your favourite band?' I asked.

'Lombardo,' he said without hesitation. 'I've seen them twice.'

'They're that underground rock band that claim to be werewolves, right?' I asked, apparently being correct because he looked impressed that I knew who they were.

Logan came over to the table and sat between us, on the table rather than on the seat. He commented on my scarf and I smiled nervously as he went to feel it as I stood up, pulling it from my neck. Most of the table gasped then started bombing me with questions.

Lorna grabbed my wrist and walked me out of the cafeteria and onto the school's front lawn. She knew that it was a vampire bite and began to grill me for details.

'I don't know what happened,' I exclaimed. 'I woke up with it.'

Lorna said something back but I didn't hear her, because his voice was in my head again.

'You're something different. I thought I was in a dream, but no. What are you? You're something new, I know that much.'

I looked around me frantically. He was here. Fear flooded me. He was here, and knew who I was! I opened my mind trying to find where he was, but too many other voices rushed in. It was too late; I couldn't close my mind again. I didn't know how to turn it off. Everyone's thoughts were flooding into mine.

I called out to Raiyn in my head as I felt my body weaken, my palms pressed to my temple. I could faintly hear Lorna asking if I was okay. In the distance, I saw Raiyn running towards me before I collapsed, and everything went silent.

# CHAPTER TWELVE

I tossed and turned, the yellow eyes again plaguing my mind. I finally woke up to the bleakness of an unfamiliar room. I could hear the rain pouring down. Looking over at the clock on the bedside table and saw it was three in the morning. I suddenly realised someone else was in the room with me. I looked to the other side of the bed and jumped when I saw someone sitting there.

'It's just me, Christopher,' he said calmly as though talking to a wild animal. 'You're in the hospital.'

I looked at him confused, not trusting what he was saying. Then I remembered the earlier hours, the bite mark, the fainting at school. That was embarrassing. Wait a second… his voice. Christopher was the vampire! I went to jump out of bed away from him only to realise I was handcuffed to the bed.

'What the hell?' I demanded. 'Since when did hospitals chain their patients in bed?'

'Your sister did that. She said if you were going to run away again she would at least deserve a goodbye this time.'

My jaw dropped. Did she really think I was just going to take off in the middle of the night? Like really? I did that once… okay twice, but I had really good reasons both times.

'Well, you can leave now then,' I snapped at Christopher.

He remained sitting beside me, staring at me. I glared at him but he didn't move so I repeated myself in case he was stupid or deaf but he still didn't move.

'I'm not leaving,' he said calmly. 'Don't worry, I won't hurt you.'

'I'm sorry if my neck and I don't trust you,' I said sarcastically.

I saw his lips thin, and I knew I had hit a nerve. Freaking vampires, so superior and stubborn. If I ever saw him out of this hospital bed I was totally going to show him who he was dealing with.

'You're not going to ask what I am?' he asked, as I determinedly looked everywhere in the room but him.

'The Animas Tenebris,' I muttered under my breath. *Shit!*

'How do you know of them?' he asked nervously.

I hesitated. I meant to say vampire! How did I explain knowing that word? 'It means souls of darkness. It's a Witches, Vampire and,' I coughed, 'ruling council, right?'

There was a third supernatural creature within the council, it was my father's species, but I didn't want him sniffing around and working out that's what I was. He enquired how I knew about them.

'That unfinished business I had?' I said, opting for the half-truth. 'I was hunting a vampire who killed my boyfriend and brother. That's why I didn't relocate with my family straight away.'

'Did you find the vampire?' he asked.

I looked into his eyes. 'How old are you?' I asked changing the subject.

He looked at me. He was obviously curious and wanted to know the whole story and what had happened but knew not to push it. He smiled and looked down.

'I was born in eighteen ninety-five,' he stated.

He was only ten years older than me. I wonder if he was in the supernatural war, and if he was, whose side had he been on. Was he on my side, or Jedhail's side?

'Aren't you worried I'll tell everyone who and what you are?' I asked.

He laughed. 'I'm pretty sure everyone would just think you're crazy.'

I smirked at him, then rolled over, determined to go back to sleep. Hopefully he wouldn't still be sitting there when I woke up. Why did he have to be a vampire? I wished he was a mere mortal now. I'd happily choose a mortal over a vampire.

I finally dozed off again, falling into an old memory, but the weird thing was, the guy I was with in the memory had Christopher's face. I didn't know him back then; however I did remember knowing a vampire family back then, their names and appearances completely forgotten to me. Was it possible for Christopher to be a part of that family? I mean it wasn't impossible…

# CHAPTER THIRTEEN

I was discharged from the hospital that morning, which I was highly thankful for. I sat up in my bed watching Raiyn, a smirk on his face, unlocking the handcuffs. I wanted to mutter "your girlfriend is crazy" but kept my mouth shut. I would have to have a word with Lorelai about this. I mean come on, I wasn't planning on running away anytime soon.

I saw Christopher standing down the hall and scowled. I'm pretty sure he heard me too because I heard him laugh softly to himself. The loser, he probably found this highly amusing. Why was he still here? I threw my legs over the side of the bed and went out of the hospital room, refusing to make eye contact with him as I walked past.

Raiyn led me to the car, where Lorelei was waiting. She handed me a bag with clothes in it so I didn't have to go to school with the same clothes as yesterday. I muttered a thanks which she chose not to acknowledge. I kept feeling Raiyn's eyes glance back at me as we drove to school.

'I'm fine,' I said, with a smile.

'I'm just worried about you A,' he said, smiling back at me. 'Did this have anything to do with the dream the night before?'

I nodded.

It was kind of because of the dream. I mean if Christopher hadn't bitten me in that stupid dream I wouldn't have gotten the scar, and if I hadn't gotten the scar, I wouldn't have had the incident at school.

'What dream?' Lorelei asked, glancing in the review mirror at me. 'Is that why you stayed in her room the other night?'

'Yeah, she woke up screaming, so I stayed with her,' Raiyn said not looking at Lorelei. We both knew I was a sore spot when it came to her. I wondered how long she'd stay angry at me for running away.

Both Raiyn and I stayed silent after that, not wanting to upset Lorelei. As we parked I noticed the newspaper on the seat beside me. There had been multiple murders lately, and this one was getting closer into town. I picked up the paper to see the photo better when a sudden flash of blood and pain flooded my entire body, I dropped the paper and found Lorelei and Raiyn both looking at me with concern.

'I'm fine,' I said with a forced smile. Noticing we were parked I stepped out of the car to get away from worried eyes. That had been weird. I had seen blood, darkness, heard screaming and the pain of dying ran though my body.

As I walked to class I noticed Christopher was waiting for me in the hallway. I chose to walk past him and sit further down the table away from him.

I was more than grateful when the bell rang, I went and sat beside Lorna in the cafeteria.

'Christopher is trying to get your attention,' Lorna whispered.

'Don't draw attention,' I hissed.

I looked over and found him looking at me. This was ridiculous. He was driving me crazy.

'I'm not feeling well,' I said to Lorna. 'I'm just going to walk home.'

I walked out of the cafeteria and out of the school grounds. I suddenly felt calmer and more relaxed than I had within the school. I started walking home, enjoying the sunshine. Hearing my name, I turned to see Christopher running to catch up with me. I rolled my eyes and kept walking, not waiting for him.

'Hey, just talk to me,' he said, stopping me in my tracks once he'd caught up.

I shot him a dirty look which just made him smirk at me. I growled under my breath and kept going. Annoyingly he walked beside me.

'You never told me your story?' he said as we walked towards my house.

Ignoring him, I kept walking. What was this, social time? "Hey, let's be friends with the vampire who bit me in my dreams." Oh god, now I was sounding crazy.

'Arya,' he said, stopping me again. 'I just need to understand how a normal girl like you got involved with vampires.'

I couldn't help but smile, he called me normal.

'I know you. What's the difference?'

He looked at me, probably trying to read my mind. Good luck! I took in his features and wondered if he was the vampire I knew all those years ago. I also wondered why I didn't remember them. I remembered many things from back then, people and all, but I couldn't place that family.

I walked off, instructing him not to follow me.

# CHAPTER FOURTEEN

It was about ten at night. I was sitting on the couch reading a book whilst my family sat at the table talking. I overheard my father say something about the murders, pulling my attention from my reading.

'What do you know about the murders?' I asked, closing my book.

'I heard about the first one the day you arrived here actually. It was just outside Versattali and now it's rather close to Skarsgard.'

'It's him,' I whispered to myself. It wouldn't be a coincidence.

'What are you talking about sweetheart?'

I looked at my parents, tears threatening to spill from my eyes. Mum came over and embraced me. She knew who I meant. These murders were my fault. I should have killed him.

'Jedhail?' my father enquired, 'I thought you…' he coughed, unable to finish the question.

I shook my head. Nefertiti sat back on the couch beside me. 'I didn't. I only got Elphina.' I whispered in shame.

'Perhaps it is Jedhail then.'

'Father, I'm so sorry I didn't…'

'No,' he interrupted. 'I never wanted you to seek revenge in the first place.'

I smiled at him, getting up to hug him, then I said goodnight to both of my parents. I walked up to Raiyn's room and knocked softly on the door. Lorelei was fast asleep but Raiyn slipped out and we went to mine.

'Do you remember the vampire family we knew in the war?' I asked as we sat on my bed.

'Vaguely, it was you who knew them best. How come?'

I sighed. 'I thought it may have been Christopher's family. I have some feeling of familiarity with him.'

'I know what you did,' Raiyn said softly changing the subject.

I looked at him, hoping he hadn't meant what I thought he'd meant. He couldn't know my darkest moment… the dark magic I used… what I did.

'I hadn't left yet. I was following your scent and I found the town, but you'd already gone.'

I looked away from him. My stomach sunk. I brushed my hands through my hair, and put my head on my knees. How do you explain the loss of control, the magic taking over your body? I felt him move closer to me, and pull me into a hug.

'I don't blame you,' he whispered. 'I love you.'

I blamed me. It was my fault. It may have been the magic getting out of control, but the magic is still me. Raiyn kissed my forehead and left my room, returning to Lorelei.

I must have been exhausted because I fell into a deep sleep. In my dream, I was back in the late seventies. I was walking the street with Rhys when I saw Christopher lurking behind a tree. Rhys's tanned skin glowed in the moonlight and his dark brown hair was styled nicely. I told Rhys to meet me back home and made my way to Christopher. As I reached him I saw his eyes linger from my tattoo down to the star shaped sapphire ring I wore.

'Where's the book?' he asked.

'Back at the house. Is that what you're here for? To see if the three things that represent my existence are safe with me?' I asked.

'No, of course not, my love,' he said, and kissed me. I felt the passion rush through me but he quickly pulled away. 'My darling Faith, I cannot stay. till next time.' He disappeared so I continued my walk home.

When I walked through the front door I sensed something wrong and saw Rhys walking down the staircase. He looked at me with disapproval.

'Was that the famous Christopher?'

I ignored his question. 'Where is my grimoire?'

'Where you always leave it,' he replied, confused.

I ran up the stairs to my room. Lorna was asleep in my bed and Mikhail asleep on the floor. I felt guilty for kissing Christopher. I ignored the feeling and went to my desk. I opened the drawer to find it empty, cursing under my breath.

I woke the next morning remembering that day. I looked at the cat on my wrist. Getting up I went to the bathroom where my ring was and I slipped in on my finger.

The tattoo represented my existence, a birth mark that forever showed my power and who I was within.

The ring protected it, and captured all my secrets and the magics I performed.

The grimoire revealed the history of my powers and my whole life story, spells and all sorts of magic I could use.

The book was impossible to read unless you had the ring, however since that day I had never got it back from Christopher. He stole it that night, and didn't see me again, it was the last kiss we shared, the last time I saw him, until the war began.

The next day at school as I was walking through the grounds, I saw Lorna. I ran up to her, pulled her aside and told her about the dream and the Jedhail murder theory.

'Do you think it's Christopher or just because he's another vampire the memoires are being triggered? Because he doesn't remember who you are either, right?'

Good theory, I thought to myself. 'What about Jedhail?'

'You're obsessed,' she grumbled. 'Why would he come after you?'

Why *wouldn't* he was the actual question. I killed his love, and I wanted him dead after he killed Rhys. I still did want him dead. I watched Lorna walk away, deciding to push the dream aside for now. I walked into class and sat down beside Logan.

As I sat, a flash like I'd gotten in the car flashed though me. This one, however, was more vivid. I saw a girl, maybe seventeen, blonde and petite. There was so much blood; she was soaked in it. The blood was coming from a wound in her neck. She was crawling away from something or someone. She was in a forest and her scream echoed in my mind. I cried out in pain, feeling her suffering.

'Valentino, are you okay?' Logan asked, his eyes full of concern.

'I've just got a headache, promise,' I said, trying to reassure him. I just wished this day would end, and I hoped I wouldn't see Christopher.

And what was with these visions?

# CHAPTER FIFTEEN

Logan and I walked to Ancient History together. I noticed he seemed nervous. Was it because of my freak out? I didn't pay too much attention to it as I was more worried about the fact that the class had a seating arrangement. When we entered, I walked to the back of the room and took my seat beside Christopher. I was glad when he didn't acknowledge me as I sat down.

I took a deep breath, one I hadn't realised I was holding, which I instantly regretted as I inhaled in his scent. Dammit. I resisted the urge to place my head on the table and close my eyes until class was over. Logan had put his books on his desk but was now walking to the back of the class to talk to me.

'Can I ask you something?' he asked.

I nodded. I needed something to distract me from Christopher. Why did he have to smell so amazing? He smelt like snow and roses. Man, I hated vampires! I wondered what I smelled like to him. Yes, that sounded weird, but I was a rare breed so I would have a unique scent, right? What is with us supernatural creatures and scent? Right, distraction, Logan was going to say something...

'So, I got tickets.' Logan paused. *Oh crap. I know where this is going.*

'Tickets?' I repeated nervously. 'For what?'

'This weekend, there is this festival on in a neighbouring town.'

'That'd be fun, the whole group going?'

Logan laughed nervously. 'No, I just have two, for you and me.'

'You mean a date?' I asked.

He nodded.

Wow, I wanted a distraction and certainly got one. I hesitated. I felt Christopher turn in my direction. Logan's eyes were on me too, but I couldn't bring myself to look at either of them.

I opened my mouth to say something but nothing came out. I didn't want to use a pathetic excuse that'd make him hate me.

'I like you as a friend,' I whispered, finally meeting his gaze. 'There's someone else.'

'Oh – I didn't realise you were seeing someone. You never mentioned,' Logan said, looking a little hurt and confused.

I was about to say I was sorry but he held up his hand to stop me.

'Don't apologise. I just wish I'd known before I'd said anything,' he said with a weak laugh. 'I better return to my seat, I'll see you at the end of class.'

I watched him walk back to his seat then closed my eyes. I rubbed my temples and sighed. I could feel Christopher looking at me but I refused to look at him. I counted the minutes till the end of the class and the second the bell rang I grabbed my books and ran out of the room.

Being in such a rush, I wasn't looking where I was going and crashed into someone, dropping all my things. I apologised and knelt down to pick up my stuff. Christopher came up from behind me and knelt picking up one of my books for me.

'What do you want?' I asked him with too much rudeness in my voice.

He looked at me, but stayed silent. I brushed my hair back and off my face, looking at him with frustration before standing up and walking off, hoping he wouldn't follow.

I went home, needing a new topic on my mind. I sat on the couch with my nose in a book, trying to distract myself. This wasn't me, I wasn't this teenage girl, this weak teenage girl. I was a powerful supernatural creature with too much attitude. So why was I falling apart?

I could feel the magic coursing through my veins, fighting the urge to be free. The monster that ripped apart Vila was just beneath my skin, caged within me. The side of me that my parents didn't know existed, the side they believed couldn't exist. If only they knew.

My parents and siblings were sitting at the dining table talking but I was barely paying attention.

'There must be a connection?' I heard Raiyn say.

'You're wrong; I've got them all here in order. They don't have anything in common,' Lorelei argued.

Curiosity got the better of me. I sighed, closing my novel, getting up and going over to the table. I started reading the files over Lorelei's shoulder.

'These are police files. How'd you get them?'

'Mum used her charm. We needed to investigate these murders,' Raiyn said.

I continued reading over Lorelei's shoulder. She was right, all six girls were different ages, different skin and hair colours, and they lived in different towns.

'Wait,' I said, re-reading the motels they had died in again. 'You said this was in order, right?'

Lorelei nodded, not paying much attention. My stomach dropped, and my heart started racing. I was trying not to hyperventilate. Was I having a heart attack?

'How could I be so foolish?' I muttered to myself with frustration.

The second girl had stayed in Krypto Hills Motel and the third girl had stayed in the Starlight Motel. I'd stayed in both of them.

'Arya?' I heard a voice say. I looked up at Raiyn, assuming he was the one that called me. He looked at me, concerned.

'It's Jedhail,' I managed to spit out.

'But didn't you?' Lorelei asked.

I shook my head, looking at the list of girls he'd killed again. He was on his way here, on his way to me.

Lorelei looked to my mother. I assumed they were both wondering the same thing. Would I leave again? I looked at Raiyn and he looked worried; probably scared I'd turn to magic again to beat Jedhail.

'Can the authorities trace it back to you?' my father asked.

'Nope,' I said, sitting on the empty chair next to Lorelei. 'I used aliases, stayed off the cameras, paid cash. They have no way of tracing me.'

'What about Hunters?' my father asked. 'I've heard they've been racking up numbers lately.'

I paused.

'I did cross paths with a Hunter,' I said without meeting his eyes.

'Just an average Hunter?' he pressed.

'No, he was from the Wyatt Hunters group. But he had no idea that I wasn't human,' I interjected.

'Are you sure?' Archer pressed.

'Yes,' I lied.

Mother put her hand on my father's. 'The Wyatt Hunters have a code. We should be safe but just in case we shall lie low for a while.'

Lorelei turned to me to say something, but changed her mind and turned back to the documents in front of her.

'Just say it, Lorelei,' I said, not looking at her, waiting for the lecture.

'Why did you come home?' she asked. 'Before you killed him.'

I looked at her, surprised by the question. I felt Raiyn and my parents also look at me. I remembered back to the night in the church.

'I slipped up,' I whispered. 'I gave him an opening to kill me but he chose to walk away. Not because he had a change of heart but because he's playing me and wasting my time. It was his way of continuing to torture me, to keep me reliving what he did. So I walked away, decided to try and move on, for Rhys.'

Lorelei and I looked at each other in silence. Raiyn put his arm around her when I turned away. Lorelei and I never got along, but we understood each other, and right now she was realising that I came home to make things the way they were. I wasn't planning on running away again.

'This is Aaron Malcolm,' my father said, breaking the silence and handing me a photo. 'The camera only caught his face in one murder, but his tattoo has been caught on film in every murder. It was a commissioned tattoo. No one else has it. I haven't even seen the symbol before.'

I looked at the tattoo and bile rose in my throat. I'd seen the tattoo before, on Jedhail. Before the war he'd told me it was his symbol for freedom. Styr's fire note had said he couldn't track the person following me because they weren't supernatural. Jedhail was smart – he'd hired a human. I stood up, the photo still in my hand.

'Just give me a minute,' I said, turning from the table and walking up to my room.

I found a map in my drawer and laid it out on the floor. I also retrieved an amethyst and tied a piece of string and the photo to it. I spun the crystal around the map, this guy was not going to hide anymore. After just a few seconds the crystal landed in Robin Falls. I smiled, satisfied. In a cloud of black smoke I teleported to where the crystal landed.

The room I stood in was almost empty. Except for a duffle bag in the corner and a bed it was bare... and dark. He'd kept all the curtains closed. I leaned against the wall and waited for my prey to return. The door opened and a scrawny young man entered. Even though the light was dull, I could see the tattoo on his wrist. His auburn hair fell down across his eyes.

'Aaron Malcolm,' I said.

He spun around looking for me. I appeared in front of him and pushed him up against the wall.

'Why are you being blamed for the murders of all those girls?' I asked harshly, holding him against the wall.

He stayed silent, but I could sense his fear. I looked into his mind. He wasn't the one killing the girls but he was ... dammit! He was blood bonded to Jedhail. Blood bound was when a vampire gave a human his blood to bind him to him. As long as the vampire lived and continued giving Aaron blood, he would never age but he'd remain human, for the most part.

I threw Aaron to the floor. 'Why are you bonded?' I yelled.

He spat at my feet. 'As long as the dark prince lives, so shall I, and I will be rewarded for my loyalty. You are a traitor.'

I crouched down before him. 'Listen to me you pathetic insect.' My voice was cold and dark. 'I will kill Jedhail, and then I will come back for you. So I suggest you pass that on to your dark prince and then run, and hope I don't find you.'

I teleported back home and arrived in the kitchen by accident. My parents looked at me with confusion and I looked at Raiyn to see disapproval. Lorelei must have gone upstairs to bed.

'Well,' I said, breaking the silence. 'Aaron Malcolm is mortal, but he's blood bonded to Jedhail. I recognised the tattoo. Jedhail has the same one.'

'You teleported,' Mum stated.

'Yes,' I replied, confused. 'I've been doing it since I was five.'

'We got the letter you were coming home weeks before you actually showed. Why didn't you teleport? You wouldn't have had anyone follow you through these hotels, you wouldn't have crossed the path of a Wyatt.'

'I was getting nightmares about Cassandra's daughter,' I explained. 'I needed to follow them.'

Raiyn stood up and asked if he could talk to me. I said goodnight to Mum and Dad and followed Raiyn upstairs to my room. He ushered me in and closed the door behind him.

'What are you doing?' he scolded. 'You finally got out of this mess. Stay out of it. I don't want Jedhail coming near you. Do you really want to go up against him again?'

For a moment, I hesitated.

*Would I fight him? Would I be able to win? Was the vendetta still contained in my blood?* The animal in me growled from within its cage and I knew I had my answer.

'I want to kill him,' I said. 'I want to make him pay. He took Rhys from me.'

'I lost him too,' Raiyn yelled. 'He was my brother longer than he was yours. I didn't run off trying to get myself killed to avenge him. And what do you think would happen to me if you lost control again and didn't come back this time? Or worse if he killed you?'

I opened my mouth to say something, but I didn't know what to say. He was right. I was the only one that got angry over Rhys's death, the rest of my family mourned him and moved on. I couldn't do that. And what would Raiyn say if he knew I didn't care if I died, but I never thought of what would happen to my family if I died. I only thought of myself. I met Raiyn's gaze, trying to say I was sorry. He was right, I hadn't thought of it that way. I was just so focused on my pain. I looked down, scared my eyes would betray me and release tears.

Raiyn turned around and stormed out of the room. I knew I should have called out to him, but I had nothing to say, nothing that he wanted to hear anyway.

# CHAPTER SIXTEEN

The next day after school I stayed back with Lorna. I was too scared to go home. Raiyn hadn't talked to me since he stormed out of my room last night. I didn't know what to say to him. I wanted to tell him I was sorry but at the same time I still needed to fight. I needed my closure, my act of revenge.

'Lorelei messaged me last night,' Lorna said as we slowly walked back to my house later that evening. I looked at her but she was avoiding eye contact. 'She said she overheard you and Raiyn arguing. She's worried you're going to run off again. And don't say you won't, I can see it in your eyes. You want to finish this. So I'm asking you as a friend, don't go.'

Well played Lorelei. Sometimes you needed someone outside of the family to give the message. It tended to get better results.

'I won't run away again,' I said honestly. I felt Lorna relax. 'But, if Jedhail comes here and confronts me, I'm going to fight. I don't have a choice.'

Lorna sighed, 'You always have a choice.'

I gave her a look that made her just roll her eyes. When we reached my house, I quickly searched for Raiyn's presence but he didn't seem to be home at the moment. I relaxed and walked inside. We went straight up to my room.

We sat on the floor creating small spells with the elements. We were creating flames and turning them into the shapes of people, making them dance and twirl. It was beautiful. We were at it for hours, not realising it was night until we looked out my window.

'Lorna, what do you know about Christopher?' I asked as our conversation began to wane.

'I don't know a lot about him personally,' she said, still making her fire figure twirl. 'But those two girls he sits with in school, they are part of a clan of seven. There's Raven, Echo, Christopher, Jarret, Ashard and Laney.

I counted the names on my fingers, 'That's only five.'

'Oh right,' Lorna said, still distracted, now turning her flame into a dragon. 'Raven had a brother in the clan. An actual brother from when they were human, but he gave up his soul before the war. That's all I really know. I only know that much because when they first came into town I investigated a little, wanted to make sure they weren't dangerous or a threat.'

Lorna's dragon spread its wings, then all of sudden she lost control of her magic and the dragon disappeared. For a moment we sat in silence and I felt a twinge of fear in the air around her. She shrugged it off and created a small flame again.

Reaching out I went to gently touch her. 'Are you okay?'

At my touch she pulled away, her flame disappearing again. 'I'm fine.'

Her skin was ice cold and she was starting to look pale. I sat forward on my knees before her. She glanced out the window and a flash of fear was reflected in her eyes but she remained silent. Hesitantly, I glanced towards the window. It was a full moon ...but it was blue.

'The ritual?' I whispered looking back at her. 'You haven't done it yet? How did you not know today was the full moon?'

'I didn't want to,' she started to say. All of a sudden, she doubled over in pain and started screaming.

Raiyn and my father ran in. I was still sitting beside Lorna as she continued to scream. Raiyn threw me backwards out of the way.

'What are you doing to her?' I tried asking.

'Get her out of here,' Raiyn shouted as he picked Lorna up and put her on my bed.

My father grabbed my arm, pulling me to my feet and out of the room. I couldn't take my eyes off Lorna but my father closed the door behind him. My heart was racing. What was happening?

'Do you know how the blue moon ritual works?' my father asked me.

I shook my head without making eye contact, but I was guessing if Lorna didn't want to do it again it must be bad.

'It's rather cruel to be honest. You seek out a pure soul, which usually means a newborn and you offer it as a sacrifice to Hecate. The witches she deems worthy get to keep their immortality till the next blue moon.'

'How do I do it?' I said without hesitation.

'Find clear water and summon the golden nymphs, they'll tell you where to find a pure soul. Then find somewhere high and summon Hecate and offer your sacrifice for Lorna's immortality; just remember that by performing the ritual you are taking a life that isn't yours to take.'

I didn't say anything. I had the images of Lorna flashing through my mind, and I knew I couldn't lose her. Without another word I ran down the stairs and into the night. The only "waters" I knew was the creek beneath the bridge coming into town. There was no doubt in my mind over what I had to do, Lorna deserved to live. When I reached the bridge I jumped over the railing into the shallow waters. Once I was in the middle of the lake I closed my eyes and listened to the silence around me. I was alone.

I spoke an enchantment. Even with my eyes closed I saw a bright light approaching, I slowly opened my eyes.

Before me stood a young girl. She looked about fifteen but I knew she would be hundreds of years old. She had fair skin and beautiful blonde hair of loose curls. She wore a thin gold dress that had a V-neck so low that it barely covered anything.

Her rose pink lips smiled at me before she spoke, her voice like a lullaby. 'Arya, what does your heart desire to know on this most beautiful night?'

'I need to find a pure soul,' I said directly.

'But you are one,' she said gently.

Huh? How could I be a pure soul? I had killed people. She smiled at my confusion.

'Your bloodline is the purest of souls. They can't be conformed only hidden beneath the consciousness.'

'What does that even mean?'

'It's like there are two wolves within us, one wolf is our soul, one wolf is our consciousness. When you embraced the dark, you gave control to your consciousness. When you relinquished the darkness, you gave the power back to your soul.'

I muttered thanks to the nymph girl before running out of the creek. Behind me I saw the light of the nymph fade and I ran as fast as my legs could take me through the forest until I reached a cliff edge.

'Hecate,' I shouted. 'I summon you to answer me right now.'

Thunder and lightning started arguing across the sky. The clouds darkened but no rain fell.

'You called, my dear?' said a cold, cruel voice from behind me.

I turned and looked upon Hecate, her long, tangled, black hair was wild in the wind and her onyx eyes looked like two black tunnels focused upon me.

'My friend…' I began.

'Yes, the witch,' she said lazily. 'Do you bring me the sacrifice for her immortality?'

There was no hesitation in my voice. 'Yes, I offer you my soul.'

Hecate laughed, her voice echoing into the sky, encouraging the thunder.

'I do not accept. Your witch is dead,' she said with a cruel smile.

'But my soul is amongst the purest,' I argued.

'Yes, but to live is torture for you, so I give you the curse of life.'

'NO!' I screamed, throwing Hecate into the darkness with a burst of violent wind.

I turned back to the cliffs edge, the lightning was flashing across the sky.

'GODDESS HECATE,' I screamed. 'TAKE MY SOUL. I OFFER MY IMMORTALITY IN EXCHANGE FOR LORNA'S! DO AS I SAY!'

Rain started to pour down so heavily that soon hail fell down at my feet. I stood there for a few moments but nothing happened. How could this happen? I failed Lorna. I hated myself for it. I couldn't let her die. I walked slowly back to the house, not knowing what else I could do.

As I stepped in the door Lorna threw herself into my arms.

'Thank you,' she whispered.

After she left my father looked at me. 'Who'd you sacrifice?'

I shook my head. 'I didn't,' I whispered. 'I tried offering my own soul but she didn't take it. I don't know why she let Lorna live?'

My father looked concerned, but quickly hid it with a soft smile and hugged me.

The next few days were fairly quiet. Lorna and I didn't speak about the blue moon incident. We both just wanted to forget it.

Friday the school was covered in fog, making me uneasy. I walked across the school grounds at the end of the day, flicking through one of my note books whilst trying to balance my other books.

'Hey Valentino,' yelled Matthew, catching up to me. I smiled to acknowledge him. 'So I was wondering if you wanted to go to dinner with me this weekend, as in a date.'

I looked up at him in complete shock, almost stumbling in my tracks. His cheeks flushed in embarrassment, so I tried to give him a comforting smile.

'Oh, Matt, hon, I don't know if that'd be a good idea. I love our friendship but trust me I'm a train wreck so I'm going to have to say no.'

'I understand,' he said with a forced smile. 'Maybe we can do something outside of school as just friends.'

'Of course, hon. Whenever. Just give me the details and I'll be there,' I said with a smile then continued across the school ground.

As I reached the sidewalk I managed to slip on the road and completely fall over. I got up quickly before anyone seemed to notice, but looking around I noticed Christopher watching me. I took a deep breath and looked away. I swear he saw me fall and was now laughing at me. Perhaps my notes could wait till I got home, I thought, shoving my books into my bag.

'Arya,' said a voice in my head. 'Come to me.'

I looked around but saw no one, so I started walking home.

'Arya, I order you to come to me.'

I stopped dead in my tracks. I recognised the voice and changed my path to walk through the forest until I came out on the cliffs edge and saw Hecate standing there with her back to me.

'You summoned,' I said lazily.

'Don't use that ungrateful tone with me child,' she snapped.

I suppressed a sigh. 'I'm sorry Goddess Hecate, thank you for saving Lorna's life.'

'It's not without a price,' Hecate said turning to me. Her black eyes sent shivers down my spine.

*Of course it isn't.* 'What is it that I owe?'

She smiled a cruel smile that made my stomach churn nervously. 'You shall not need to know that just yet. I will find you when I need you. Until then, enjoy your immortality, won't you.'

And with a cold echoing laugh she disappeared.

# CHAPTER SEVENTEEN

In a spare room of the house my parents had set up a small dedication to Rhys, though I had not yet been in it. I was too scared to enter. I took a deep breath and walked to the door. My fingers gently touched the door handle, but they only stayed there for a moment. I pulled away, feeling an unbearable pain in my chest.

I had to pull myself together, this was ridiculous.

Again my fingers reached out and took hold of the door handle. This time I ignored the pain and pushed the door open. The room was basically empty, except for a piano and above it a photo of Rhys. I looked into his deep brown eyes, his pale pink lips were almost closed with a small smile. He looked in his early twenties with his little amount of facial hair, and his chocolate brown hair was brushed back off his face, probably blowing in the wind when this had been taken.

On the piano there was a photo of him and I. I remembered this time. It was a summer up at the lake house. Rhys had been sitting against a tree while I lay with my head in his lap. We were looking into each other's eyes. I was maybe fifteen here.

I closed my eyes remembering the conversation we had been having.

'Why do I never meet any of your girlfriends?' I had asked.

'Because I don't have any,' he replied with a smile, stroking my hair back from my face.

'But I see how girls look at you when we're out; you dazzle them.'

'Yes, perhaps, but I don't need a girlfriend.'

'Why not?' I enquired.

'Because you are the most important girl in my life,' he said, following with the most amazing smile.

I felt a tear fall down my cheek as the memory faded.

I went further into the room, letting the door close behind me. I walked over to the piano and sat on the chair, running my fingers over the keys, imagining that Rhys was playing, imagining his voice singing to me like he used to. I played the song he used to sing me to sleep with.

*Fall asleep. Fall asleep.*
*To the land you are the queen.*
*Fall asleep. Fall asleep.*
*Dream away all that haunts your mind.*

*Fall asleep. Fall asleep.*
*I'll be here when you wake.*
*Here by your side.*
*Always.*

He always spoke this last word, and then would kiss me on the forehead and tuck me in.

Rhys had taught me how to play when I was younger, but this was the first time I'd played since I'd lost him.

'It's good to see you do that again.'

I jumped and turned around to see Raiyn standing in the doorway. I hadn't heard him come in.

'You know you're the first person to come in here,' Raiyn said as he came and sat down beside me.

I looked at him, biting my lip to hold in the tears.

'I'm sorry,' I whispered.

Raiyn looked at me. I saw that he hurt too.

'We all miss Rhys. I know you miss him the most but he wouldn't let you do this to yourself, Arya. What you're doing? He would stop you if he was still here.'

'Maybe,' I said, looking away. 'If it had been me that died what do you think he would have done?'

Raiyn faltered. 'He would have torn the world apart until you were avenged,' he admitted. 'He loved you more than life itself.'

He stood up and kissed my hair before turning on his heels and left me in silence. I stayed motionless until I heard the door click into its lock. Turning to look at the closed door I wondered, *would he have gone to the same extent for revenge as I have?*

I needed to know.

Without another thought, I stood up from the piano and ran out of the room and into my own bedroom, falling to my knees before my bed. From underneath I pulled out an elegantly carved wooden chest made from chestnut. As I opened it a soft aroma of mixed fragrances overwhelmed my senses. It was my potions chest, containing all my ingredients. Thinking of the spell I needed I removed a crystal jar containing red sand, five white candles, a small aluminium basin, a silver knife, a feather of an owl, salt, cat nip, hyacinth, lavender and marjoram.

I placed the basin before me and made a circle around it with the red sand. Just inside the sand line I placed the candles so if I played connect-the-dots it would make a pentagram.

'Accendo,' I muttered with a wave of my hand and the candles set alight.

'Pluma de noctuae,' I whispered as I placed the feather of the owl in the basin.

'Nepeta Cateria.' I threw the cat nip in.

'Hyacinth, Lavender, Marjoram.'

Picking up the knife I pressed it to my finger, breaking the skin, pushing down on my finger over the basin so a drop of blood fell onto the ingredients.

'Sanguine ut oblation,' I whispered as I placed the knife back on the floor beside me.

'Power of the witches rise. Course unseen across the skies. Take me back to where I'll find, what I wish in place and time,' I said aloud and threw a pinch of salt into the basin.

Nothing happened.

'NO!' I shouted, throwing more than a pinch of salt in the basin. This time a deafening wind burst into my room, throwing me against the wall. When I opened my eyes I wasn't in my room anymore. I was at a party in my old house. I was still me, but wore a beautiful blue corset and long black pants with a long sash and silver metal buckle. I'd worn this before, but where? I took in the environment around me, a rainbow of colours from boutique corsets and suits. The scent of too many bottles of wine lingered in the room. The piano was playing.

*RHYS!*

This was the night he had died. I frantically looked around the room for him, ignoring those trying to talk to me. I'd searched the entire party, he wasn't there; I ran until I reached the staircase. I knew it was wrong to change history but I couldn't let him die. I ran upstairs as fast as my legs would take me; I'd forgotten how uncomfortable it was in a corset. Without a moment's thought or memory, I busted into his room and was grabbed by someone.

*No, this can't happen again. I can't watch him die again.* Jedhail stood before me holding Rhys.

'No, please let him go,' I yelled, struggling against whoever held me.

And just like deja vu, before my eyes Jedhail's fangs sank into Rhys's throat. I couldn't hear myself screaming but I knew I was as I watched horror-struck. And just like last time, I heard Rhys's neck snap beneath Jedhail's hands. I was released and ran to Rhys, falling before his body.

'No, please!' I cried. 'I need you. I'm so sorry. I'm sorry I couldn't save you.'

I blinked, waking up back on my bedroom floor, my heart pounding against my chest.

# CHAPTER EIGHTEEN

It was the middle of the night and I lay on my bed listening to music, trying to distract my mind as I stared at the ceiling. I dozed off to sleep and found myself in a familiar place but I was aware that I was only dreaming. I was near the forest just outside of town. What was I doing here?

I saw a young, blonde girl ahead of me. She was on her morning run. Jedhail walked out of the forest and grabbed the girl from behind. I screamed out to her but I couldn't move. I had to watch as he sunk his teeth into her neck. Her screams woke me.

I looked at the clock on my bedside table and saw it was five in the morning. I grabbed my jacket and ran out of the house towards the bridge that led into town. My body argued at running this early in the morning in the cold without a warm up but I didn't slow down. As I reached the place I'd seen in my dreams I found I was too late. There were cops and a crowd of other morning runners. I walked over to the girl's body, it was the girl I'd seen in my dream. I looked into the forest and my eyes met Jedhail's. He smiled at me before disappearing amongst the trees.

Looking around to make sure no one else noticed, I followed him into the forest. His scent brought up old memories. I followed it until the sun came up and knew it was pointless. He would be underground somewhere by now. I made my way back to town.

Later that day, during recess, Lorna and I sat outside away from the rest of the group so we could talk about what had happened.

'So you knew she was dead before you saw her body?' Lorna asked.

'I dreamt it,' I explained, while lying on the table soaking up the sun. Lorna sat on the seat beside me.

'Is premonition a part of your magic or is it just your connection to him?'

'I hope it's to do with him' I said, covering my eyes with my arm. 'Means all I have to do is kill him to make it stop.'

Though part of me didn't believe it'd stop after I killed him. Before I stopped aging I used to have dreams. I remember my first one was when I was ten, I dreamt that a village girl who got accused of being a witch was burnt alive, and the next day when I went into the village I saw it happen for real. I was glad when I stopped getting those dreams. I hoped they weren't back permanently.

I went back to the bridge that night; I stood where the girl died until it began to rain. Turning around to start the walk home I sensed someone near. I could feel him. I turned to see Jedhail's dark, brooding figured approaching me.

'Tell me lover,' he said mockingly. 'Why did you stop our little game?'

'I got bored of you running,' I snarled.

Jedhail laughed and stepped closer to me. He leaned in so his lips were beside my ear. 'I ran so you could chase me.' He kissed my neck, making me jump back.

'Why did you blood bond a human?' I asked, changing the topic.

'I didn't want other people chasing after me,' he said with a smirk upon his lips.

'Don't lie to me, you could have killed them without being caught on camera. What are you playing at?'

He ignored my question and flashed his fangs at me. 'Do their screams still haunt you?'

He disappeared into the forest leaving me standing there, replaying his question in my mind. I sensed someone behind me, I turned to find myself staring at Christopher, who did not look happy. Without saying anything to him, I walked past him in the direction of my house. I wanted nothing more than to have a boiling hot shower to wash what just happened off me.

'What do you think you're doing?' Christopher fumed, catching up to me. 'Why were you with him? Why would you let him touch you?'

'Do you know him?' I demanded, stopping in my tracks.

'Answer my questions,' he snarled.

'Bite me, oh wait, you already have.' I kept walking, resisting the urge to yell at him as he fell into step beside me again. He walked with me all the way back to my house.

'I want to know how you found my mind,' he said, grabbing my wrist before I could enter my house.

'What are you talking about?' I snapped.

'That first night we spoke, I was reading and you spoke to me.'

'Tell me how you know Jedhail and I'll tell you how I spoke to you.'

Christopher glared at me then walked off. He knew something about Jedhail and I was going to find out what.

# CHAPTER NINETEEN

The question from the night before replayed in my head as I stood in my bathroom getting ready for school. How did I access his mind?

I'd let Jedhail get too close yesterday. When he was kissing my neck I should have put a knife through his heart. Why didn't I? Letting him live was a betrayal to Rhys.

I left for school, wanting to find Christopher. Walking into class I was glad to see he was already in his seat.

'What do you know about Jedhail?' I asked when I reached his table.

He looked up at me. 'It's complicated,' he said softly. 'Let's just say he's not someone to get involved with.'

I wasn't happy with that answer. 'I want you to tell me,' I spat.

'Fine,' he snapped. 'You tell me how you know him and I'll tell you my story.'

I glared at him and walked out of class, who needed to know about the English language anyway. I walked down the hall to the girls' bathroom and threw my bag in the first sink. I began pacing the bathroom. What was Christopher hiding? Was he an enemy, an associate of Jedhail?

I felt the power before I saw the person. I turned to find the hologram of Aubrey, King of Alesmera.

'What do I owe this visit?' I asked, my guard up.

He clicked his tongue, impatient with my rudeness.

'Ariella is going to succeed. Stop her, because I can guarantee you'll both lose valuable things if she doesn't get out of my kingdom.'

Smirking I turned to face the mirror, pulling out a lip balm I started applying to my lips. When it was back in my pocket, I looked at him through the mirror.

'I will go to Ariella, but not to stop her, to assist her.'

Aubrey snarled, vanishing from sight, allowing me to return to my thoughts.

The bell rang, breaking me from my thoughts. I left the bathroom and went and met up with Logan and Missy on the lawn at recess.

'This murderer is getting closer to town and no one is doing anything about it,' Logan complained. 'I mean it could be one of us next.'

'I really doubt it,' Missy replied.

I looked at her with confusion. Lorna came over and sat beside me.

'Well he said one of us could be next, right?' she said, having seen my look of confusion. 'But it won't be him or Matt. It's only girls.'

'Oh right,' I said casually. 'I don't think he'll come after you.'

'What makes you think it's a guy?' Logan asked.

Woops, I should start thinking before I speak. I forgot I can't talk to them about these things. I was wracking my brain for an explanation but I was blanking.

'Because it's more common for guys to go on killing sprees than girls,' Lorna interjected.

'I wonder how this whole massacre thing will end?' Missy enquired, ending the conversation.

Lorna and I exchanged glances, both thinking the same thing. However, I didn't get to finish my thought as I heard my name being called. I turned to see Christopher standing behind me.

'I wish he said my name,' Missy mumbled as I got up and walked out of eavesdropping range with him.

'I'm sorry about this morning,' he said. 'How about we hang out later this week and I'll share with you what I can.'

I smiled and hugged him, which surprised him.

'Thank you,' I whispered, my hand still on his arm. He smiled at me, and I suddenly got a nervous feeling.

Lorna walked home from school with me and grilled me for details. She was insistent on the fact that Christopher had feelings for me.

'It's not like that,' I argued. 'He knows something about Jedhail and he's going to tell me.'

'Why couldn't he tell you that at school?' she asked. 'Why do you have to specifically hang out for him to tell you? I'm telling you, it's a date.'

Lorna waved goodbye when we reached my house and I was secretly glad because my head was now pounding. I closed the door behind me and pressed my hands to my temples. I took a few steps forward when my mind felt like it had exploded. I got thrown back and hit the door with a shock from the pain. I ended up crouching on the ground, watching and feeling the pain of another girl being murdered by Jedhail.

The brunette screamed as he sunk his fangs into her neck, as she went limp he just dropped her to the ground. Jedhail looked around. I recognised the place, it was where he found me the other day.

'Arya, what happened?' Raiyn asked, running down the stairs towards me.

I looked at him then jumped to my feet, pulling the front door back open and running out into the street. I could hear Raiyn running behind me, trying to catch up. I ran to the spot I'd seen in my mind, but again I was too late. I fell back into Raiyn who pulled me away from the body.

'We need to do something,' I demanded.

Raiyn turned me to face him, 'It's too late, she's dead. We have to go before someone finds us here.'

Raiyn forced me to look away from the body and walked me back home.

We sat outside the front door in silence, my head on my knees and my hands in my hair. Raiyn sat beside me, his presence a comfort.

'Want to talk about it?' he asked.

I tilted my head so I could see him. 'I keep seeing the murders,' I whispered weakly. 'It's like Rhys; I keep watching Jedhail kill but can never stop it or save them. I couldn't save him...'

# CHAPTER TWENTY

I was sitting beneath a tree in the school grounds the next day reading, waiting for the bell to ring for class.

'Yo! New girl!' I looked up and standing before me was a girl that was obviously obsessed with the colour black. Her eyes looked like a racoon's from what I could see of them as she had her hair covering half her face.

'What? Has the goth queen come to give me her welcome?' I said with a snide smile, looking behind her at the other girls in black and hair across their face.

'Ha-ha, very funny new girl.'

'What do you want?' I asked, standing up.

'You bagged Christopher,' she said with a spark of jealousy in her eyes. 'How? I've been after him since he showed up in town.'

'For one, he can see my face,' I said sarcastically.

'You laugh now but he'll kill you when he's bored of you. He's a child of the night, like me. He'll make me into what he is.'

I glared at her, as she smirked at me, thinking she'd made her case. She walked back to her friends and I watched as she started talking to them, telling them what had just happened.

'Hey, Arya, isn't it?' said a sweet voice.

I turned around to see one of the girls Christopher sat with. Her hair looked redder out in the sun.

'Raven, right?' I asked as we walked over to a table and sat down.

'I hear my brother asked you out on a date?'

I looked at her, confused. Was I the only one that didn't know it was a date?

'What are you?' she asked before I could answer. 'I know you're not human, but don't worry, I haven't told anyone yet.'

'I can't reveal that just yet,' I said softly.

She accepted that answer and started asking more simple things, like how I liked the town and school. We kept talking even after the bell rang. Obviously neither of us cared about attending school properly. We spent the hour wandering the grounds.

'Did you need us to go in the shade?' I asked.

Raven shook her head. 'No, I fed this morning so I can spend some time in the sun, plus there's always enough cloud cover here that is isn't too uncomfortable. You're not going to tell anyone what you know about us, right?'

I shook my head and smiled at her.

'Is that because you have something to hide as well?' she asked.

But I didn't get to answer because Christopher approached us, not looking very happy at Raven. She smirked at me then ran off as Christopher came and sat beside me.

'Why did you spend the afternoon with my sister rather than be in class?' he asked.

'Sorry, Dad,' I said sarcastically. 'Why do you care?'

'Because she is a vampire,' he said as though it was the obvious answer.

'What's your point? You're a vampire. And why does everyone think us hanging out is a date?'

He smiled at me and kissed my cheek. 'I'll come by your place tomorrow.'

***

The next morning the heat of the sun woke me up, rather than my bad dreams for once. I looked at the time; it was nearing midday. I groaned. I supposed I had better get up. Christopher would probably be on his way over soon. The wind blew through my open window and the scent of the forest called to me. My eyes flashed green, the colour they were when I was in animal form.

I smiled devilishly. Christopher could wait. I was going to stretch my legs.

I walked out into my backyard and stripped off all my clothes. There was no point transforming in the clothes and risk ripping them all. My eyes turned from blue to green, fur came out of my skin and my bones changed inside me, transforming me into a large black cat. I stretched out my legs and swung my tail with excitement before running into the forest.

I spent the day running through the woods in my black panther form. The forest began to darken before the sky did and I decided I should probably venture home. I transformed as I reached my backyard, putting on my bra and underwear as I snuck through the back door, surprised to find Christopher sitting with Raiyn in my lounge room.

Raiyn looked over my appearance and I could tell he'd guessed what I'd been doing. I held up a finger indicating I'd be just a moment and ran upstairs to quickly shower.

I'd managed to make myself look decent in under ten minutes. I ran back downstairs and glared at Raiyn who was trying not to laugh at me.

'Shall we go?' I asked Christopher, indicating towards the front door.

He nodded and followed me outside. We walked in silence and I wondered if he found it as awkward as I did.

'What'd you do this afternoon?' he asked, remembering my appearance as I came through the back door. My hair was in every direction and with leaves, twigs, mud covering my skin.

'I just went for a run and then got some sun,' I replied. Technically I wasn't lying.

As we approached his house I was dreading the possibility of Raven outing me or one of the others picking up my scent and realising I wasn't human. However my thoughts were interrupted when I saw his house. It was an old fashioned white marbled mansion surrounded by trees. The majority of the walls held multiple windows, but the front door was a dark oak which stood out, considering the rest of the house was white.

We stepped into an empty living room and he led me over to the couch. I went to ask him about Jedhail but Raven ran down the stairs. She came over to me and hugged me. A man that looked like a body builder walked in behind her. He introduced himself as Jarret, Echo's boyfriend.

'So, tell us about humanity?' Echo said coldly, skipping her own introduction, as she walked down the stairs.

Raven nudged her as she reached her.

Echo's faced softened. 'I actually would like to know,' she said honestly.

'You wish you were human?' I said, more as a fact that a question as I read the emotions coming off of her. The same emotions that I hid within me.

She nodded. 'I have no regrets meeting Jarret but I hate being this creature.'

'How'd you turn?' I asked, knowing I could be walking on thin ice.

'I was out walking one night. My parents had arranged a marriage for me, but the guy was horrible so I snuck out. I was attacked in the street. Jarret came to my rescue but it was too late.'

Raven sat down next to me on the couch, between her and Christopher. The other two sat on the couch across from us. Raven looked me over as though deciding whether or not she trusted me.

'Christopher said you were asking questions, so I'm going to tell you our very brief history and I hope that will be enough to answer them,' Raven said.

'What did he say?' I asked.

'He said you were curious about us,' Raven said, getting comfortable in her seat. 'Ashard and Laney are the oldest. They were newly married when they got turned but they didn't stay with the vampire that turned them, they ventured off on their own. They met Jarret who was actually seeking out vampires because he was dying of a very cruel disease at that time. Christopher was shot for trying to steal food to feed his siblings. Then my brother and I were orphans, living on the street and they took us in, turning us when we turned seventeen.'

'Where's your brother?' I asked.

Raven looked sad, and I could feel the pain flowing off her in waves. 'My brother, Jedhail, gave up his soul.'

I almost choked. Jedhail was her brother! I stood up in a flash and took a step away from the couch. Raven looked at me, confused. I looked to Christopher who gave me a look saying *you wanted to know.* I apologised to Raven and ran out of the house and into the forest.

I kept running until their scent was completely out of range.

'Did you not recognise my family?' Jedhail said from behind me, making me jump.

Now that I looked at him again I could see the resemblance between him and Raven. I wondered if he'd gone to see her, if he missed her, if he felt sadness when he thought of her, like she did with him.

He walked over and stood before me. I met his gaze and watched as he pulled out a small knife and cut across his wrist.

'If you want the truth…' he said, offering me his wrist.

I looked away. Out of the corner of my eye I watched him bring his wrist to his mouth and consume his own blood. He suddenly grabbed me and kissed me. The taste of his blood lingered in my mouth when he pulled away. I went to yell at him but images entered my mind.

It was Christopher who sought me out, even though I was with Mikhail. It was Christopher who stole my grimoire. Jedhail was hunting Christopher. That's how he found me. Jedhail smirked at me then walked away. I licked the remaining blood from my lips.

# CHAPTER TWENTY-ONE

I didn't go home that night. I sent Raiyn a fire note that I needed to get away for a night or two, but I promised I'd be home soon. I decided to go to Alesmera. I'd felt some distress from Ariella lately.

I teleported to Styr's doorway and stepped through the blue door in the forest. When I entered the boring, old room I was surprised not to find Styr waiting. He mustn't have sensed me coming. He came out of the other room and looked at me with a small look of surprise. Even though he sensed me crossing over, he was shocked that I'd decided to cross over.

'Your Majesty,' he said with a small bow of his head. 'How may I assist you?'

'Let me out at the castle,' I said.

He looked at me hesitantly but agreed to my wishes, opening a doorway that I stepped through after thanking him. I found myself standing before Jareth's castle doors; I was surprised to find it without guards. I looked back and saw Jessica pacing before the black forest, probably waiting for Ariella to make it through.

I entered the castle, turning right. I knew where Jareth's room was and that's where I was going. If he wasn't there I would wait for him. I found his door and sensed him to be inside. I looked down at what I was wearing, jeans and a shirt. I stripped off the shirt, glad to see I'd worn the black lace bra today. I opened the door and closed it behind me, dropping the shirt beside me.

Jareth had his nose in a book and I saw him sigh in anger as the door closed.

'I thought I asked not to be interrupted,' he snapped, dropping the book as he froze when he saw me.

I smiled at him. He leapt off the bed.

'What are you doing here?' he asked in a less cruel tone.

I walked over to him slowly, his eyes watching me like a hawk until I reached him. I felt him tensing, as though unsure and nervous at what I'd do. I got up on my toes and kissed him. I felt him relax and wrap his arms around me, pulling me closer to him. I unbuttoned his shirt and pushed it off his shoulders, letting it fall to the floor.

I pushed him onto the bed and lay over him, kissing him again.

'I love you,' he whispered.

'I know,' I whispered back before kissing him again. Every time we did this he told me he loved me, but I never said it back, because I didn't love him, not that way anyway. Not anymore. I used to love him, when I first met him, before his father put too much influence on him.

***

I lay in his arms listening to him talk about his mum. He missed her. He talked about his favourite memories with her, and I laughed seeing there was still some good in him. His father hadn't fully erased it. He'd taken Jareth from his mum when he was only sixteen years old, raised him as his heir, never letting him see her again.

'Jedhail is stalking me,' I said to him, my chin on his chest.

Jareth stroked my hair. 'You should invest in protection, not that you need any.'

I laughed. 'What kind of protection are you suggesting?'

He shrugged. 'Dead blood is always handy against his kind.'

'That's perfect' I said, kissing him, his arms wrapped around me.

'How do you feel about me?' he asked.

I looked into his eyes and stroked his face. 'Remember when I first met you, when you were with your mum still?'

He nodded.

'I was falling in love with you, but then you left. Now all we have are these moments.'

There was a knock on the door.

'Your father wishes a meeting with you,' said the guard from outside.

Jareth tensed before getting out of bed. I watched him change, his demeanour going from relaxed back to tense and cold. He walked out of the room without looking back at me.

I jumped out of bed and realised that he had hidden my clothes. I looked down at my lace bra and underwear. I sighed, better than nothing, I stole one of his weapon belts which I wrapped around my waist, pulled my boots on and grabbed a bow and some arrows, throwing them over my shoulder as I walked out of the room.

I felt a twinge of pain and knew Ariella was injured. I ran out of the castle before teleporting to a location near her. I went over to where she was and told the guy leaning over her to move. He must have recognised me because he stepped aside without a word. I pulled two sachets out of the weapons belt I'd stolen, handing them to the guy standing behind me.

'Crush this within water, it's Gotu Kola. It'll speed up the healing process,' I ordered as I put Aloe Vera on some of her other wounds.

'You're not meant to be here,' Ariella said softly through her pain.

I looked at her, surprised she remembered that detail in this moment. 'I sensed your pain, you needed medical help,' I told her.

When the guy she was with handed me the bowl, I grabbed her knife and cut my hand, letting some of my blood fall into the bowl. I took some of the crushed leaves and pressed them into Ariella's knife wound. She cried out in pain which made me cringe. Once I knew she was taken care of I got to my feet and left, ignoring her pleas for me to stay.

I returned to Styr's room to find him waiting for me. I braced myself for bad news. I grabbed one of his robes and wrapped it around me.

'They found Elphina's bones,' he said.

# CHAPTER TWENTY-TWO

Elphina's bones were gone, Jedhail was in town stalking me, and Christopher was the reason Jedhail had destroyed my life.

*And Christopher might still have my grimoire,* I thought as I walked back into town.

He'd be at school now, so I walked to his house. When I reached it, I knocked on the door but no one answered, so I picked the lock and slipped inside. I walked upstairs realising I didn't know which room was his, opening the first room and saw a soft toy on the bed and hoped it wasn't his. None the less, I rummaged through the wardrobe. Moving onto the next room, I saw it was a library. Betting this was it. I slipped in, closing the door behind me.

I walked over to his desk, going through the drawers first. Nothing. I walked over to the wall which was just a giant book shelf. *This may take a while.* I thought as I started at one side, reading every title, making my way along the wall.

'What do you think you're doing?' said a voice behind me. I turned to see Raven standing in the door way. I ignored her and kept skimming the bookshelf till I found it. I smiled as I pulled it out, feeling the book's energy react to my touch.

'Just taking back what's mine,' I said as I walked out of the room, past her, flashing her the grimoire.

She followed me downstairs and out the door. I wondered why I didn't remember them, what spell had I cast to make that happen. I'm sure the grimoire would tell me.

'Faith,' she called out as I walked across the yard.

I turned back to her. She ran out of the house over to me so she didn't have to shout.

'What are you?' she asked. 'I never managed to work it out.'

I shrugged and turned away from her again.

'I can smell him on you, Jedhail. He's here for you, isn't he?'

I ignored her but she grabbed my wrist and the world dissolved before our eyes.

*'Don't leave me,' Christopher yelled. But it wasn't Christopher from this era, it was from the war. I stood beside a blue dragon. Christopher stood behind me with Raven.*

*'Arya, we have to go,' said Rhys who was already mounted on his black dragon.*

*'I love you,' Christopher whispered. 'Don't fight, please.'*

*'Stop saying that,' I said with frustration. 'You didn't love me, just the idea of me. You wanted my history and my power. That's why you took my grimoire.'*

*'That's not true,' he demanded. 'We just needed to know what Jedhail wanted from you, I was trying to protect you. Don't go, leave with us. We can be together.'*

*'Screw you,' I shouted. 'I don't love you. And I'm going to win this war, and destroy everyone who threatens my family!' I mounted the blue dragon. 'Goodbye Christopher,' was the last thing I said before flying off into the night with Rhys by my side.*

I snatched my wrist out of Raven's grip. As I walked away I wondered how long Raven would keep what she knew quiet, or was she looking for Christopher now to fill him in?

I walked to the town border and found a small motel. The receptionist was a middle-aged man with circular glasses and an awkward comb over. Any observer could tell he was a klutz with the amount of stains on his shirt.

'Excuse me, I would like a room, just one night.'

'Yes, Miss. Under what name shall I put that?' he asked in a husky voice.

'Kylie Patterson,' I said with a smile, handing him cash from my wallet.

As I reached the room's door an old woman pulled me aside. She looked ghastly, almost as bad as she smelled. She was covered in dirt and dust, and had a hood over her face trying to hide her features.

'Don't take the blood, it will consume you. It will be the death of you as you walk into your past,' she said, her voice weary like that of an old gypsy.

'I'm sorry about that, Miss,' said a young man in a white jacket, as he ran over to us, steering the old lady away from me. 'She is one of our schizophrenic patients; she means no harm.'

'Is there a hospital around here?' I asked.

'No, up in Kierra there's one. We're moving her from the Starlex one. It had a small fire a few weeks ago, so we're moving the patients,' he explained.

'I didn't hear about that. Did you lose any of the patients?'

'None of them died if that is what you're asking. We have misplaced one, so if you come across a Daniel Malcolm please call the authorities.'

Jedhail must have set the fire, perhaps an insane person was more useful to him than a sane person. Or a better scapegoat for murder.

Turning back to the old lady, I watched her eyes, which were wandering, she couldn't look anywhere for more than a second. Though when she spoke to me her eyes were so focused like she was certain on every word.

'Miss?' the man in white questioned. 'Are you okay?'

'Yes,' I said, dragging my gaze away from her. 'Just what she said.'

'She isn't in her right state of mind. You can't believe anything she says.'

'Are you saying that nothing they say ever comes true?' I argued.

He looked over my expression for a moment and I noticed his hesitation before answering.

'Their minds aren't right. They don't know what's going on.'

I nodded with a small smile and stepped into my room. Before closing the door, I turned back and called out, 'Excuse me, Daniel Malcolm. Was he dangerous?'

'Violent outburst wise, no, he isn't. He was weak minded. He was admitted for kidnapping a young girl and when we asked him why he did it, he said his Master ordered him to. If you find him alone, he won't be a danger.'

Forcing a smile, I closed the door, locking the door behind me. I heard the lady begin talking again, telling him the same things that she had told me. I pushed my body away from the door, I didn't want to hear anymore. I went into the bathroom and turned on the shower. Undressing, I stepped in, putting the water on much hotter than I usually would. I closed my eyes, leaning on the cool tile walls as the hot water washed over my skin.

I heard my door open and close. I left the shower on but grabbed my underwear and shirt, pulling them on. I stepped out into the bedroom, but no one was there. As I went to return to the shower someone grabbed me and pushed me up against the wall.

'You're not trying to run again, are you?' Jedhail said, his body pressed up against mine. He pressed his hands against my mouth and sunk his teeth into the flesh above my collar bone. I screamed and kneed him in the groin. He doubled over, giving me the opening to knee him in the face. He fell on the floor laughing, my blood smeared on his teeth. I pinned him to the floor, the memory of his blood flashed through my mind. I growled, my eyes flashing green and my cat teeth coming out. I leaned down and sunk my teeth into his neck.

I felt his fingers wrap around mine. I suddenly got the sick sense he was enjoying this. Pulling back from him, I slapped his face. I stood up and teleported to the other side of the room away from him.

'Get out,' I snarled.

# CHAPTER TWENTY-THREE

I awoke in a dimly lit room. Rolling over, I looked at the clock on the bedside table. It read that it was early afternoon. Why was it dark? I got up and walked to the window and peered outside to find it raining. I flicked on the light and turned around, gasping at the sight that lay before me. The bed sheets were covered in blood, and on the wall, was a message written in blood.

*'Was it good for you too?'*

I ran over to the wall and put my hands up to it, when I noticed my arms were also covered in blood. I looked down; my whole body was. But it wasn't my blood. Wait, it couldn't be blood. I would have smelt blood. I licked some of the red substance off my arm and gagged. It was paint. I knew it was Jedhail that had written the message on the wall but why? I grabbed all of my belongings and wiped my finger prints off everything in the room before running outside. As I breathed in the outside air I was hit with the aroma of blood. I looked to the room next to mine, noticing the door was slightly ajar. Pushing it open with my shoe, I threw my hand over my mouth as I saw the goth girl lying on the floor, blood still flowing from her neck.

I ran away from the motel as fast as my legs could take me, the rain washing the blood from my skin. When I got to my house I ran straight upstairs to my room, not noticing if I passed anyone. I pulled my clothes off and jumped into the shower, scrubbing my skin clean.

When I emerged I found Lorna sitting on my bed.

'Where have you been?' she asked.

I leaned against the wall and met her gaze. 'I went to see Jareth.'

She visibly relaxed. 'I thought you were going to say you went to find Jedhail.'

'I didn't have to,' I said, still not feeling clean enough. 'He found me last night.'

I offered my hand to Lorna and opened my mind, allowing her to watch the events of the evening before, from him ambushing me when I came out of the shower, to him biting me, to me biting him and how I had woken up. When the memory ended, she looked at me, shocked and horrified. I drew back my hand and closed my mind. Lorna sat in silence for a moment, looking like she had a million questions.

'What was his blood like?' was the question she chose.

'Intoxicating,' I said, more to myself than to her.

'What made you take his blood?'

I cleared my throat. 'He found me the other night at Christopher's and offered me some of his blood, to draw back the curtain. I wanted more.'

'What did he show you?'

'He's Raven's brother. It was because of my affair with Christopher that he found me.'

'Wait, they are the family you knew back then?'

I nodded. Lorna could tell I didn't want to talk anymore so she let herself out so I could rest. Hopefully I would have a more restful sleep tonight, and not wake up to a horrifying surprise. I lay in bed hoping for a dreamless sleep.

***

I felt his lust before I heard their screams.

Jedhail's memories flooded into my head, erasing my dream of a remote island and a sexy redhead worshipping me. His images filled my consciousness. He stood in the corner watching the goth girl from my school attempting to perform some sort of ritual. I was suddenly stuck standing in a glass box, I felt liquid rising. As it reached my stomach I noticed it was blood, I tried to move but was immobilised. As it rose above my head I took one last breath. A scream echoed in the back of my mind as the blood drowning me vanished.

The memory suddenly went to the first time I had met him.

*I was lying in a meadow a few streets from our house in Versattali.*

*'I don't think it's natural to sun bake in clothes,' said a voice.*

*I opened my eyes and above me stood a male in black. I quickly scrambled to my feet and stood before him.*

*'I recognise you,' I whispered. 'You're the one that has been following me.'*

*He shrugged with a malevolent look on his face.*

*'I have an offer I've wanted to present you with,' he said with a purr in his voice.*

*'I'm not interested,' I snapped turning to walk away.*

*Jedhail grabbed my arm and pulled me to him. 'You will hear what I want to propose,' he scolded.*

*I broke away from his grip and put distance between us.*

*'As you know, Arya,' I wanted to ask him how he knew my name but allowed him to continue speaking, 'there is a war brewing within the supernatural realm. I am here to warn you, you are fighting on the wrong team. Join us. It would be a shame to kill you and put your powers to waste.'*

*'Like I said before,' I spat, 'I'm not interested'.*

*'This isn't an offer you have a choice in,' he snarled.*

*'You have no power over me, not you and not anyone else,' I scoffed, coming across a bit too confident. 'I will fight for the team I want to fight for, which, unfortunately for you isn't your team. I think the reason you want me on your side, is because no-one on your side can defeat me, and you know it,' I snarled, cockiness rising in my voice. 'Now stop following me.' I flashed my green eyes before walking away.*

*'You will regret this!' he yelled after me. 'I will make you pay for turning me down!'*

The memory faded and Jedhail's voice echoed in my mind, 'I told you, you would regret it.'

I woke up, my heartbeat racing. My long hair stuck to my body which was now soaked with sweat from the nightmares. I looked at the time. It was only three in the morning. I remembered what Jareth had said about acquiring some protection.

I pulled out the chest from under my bed, digging out my silver rosary. Each bead was pure silver and blessed in holy water. I placed the rosary around my neck and tucked it into my singlet. I pulled out my crystal knife and smirked. If I got my hand on some dead blood, I could magically insert the blood into the crystal.

I hid the knife in my bag and pulled the strap over my shoulder. I needed to get some blood. I left the house and wandered into town looking for the coroner's office. The coroner had just gotten in as I arrived. I pretended to be a med student to trick him into letting me in.

'We don't have any jobs available at the moment,' he said.

'I understand that, Sir,' I said as I rummaged through my bag. I handed him a fake medical student resume and my fake student credentials. 'It's just that I am nearing the end of my degree, and I am unsure if I want to apply for a job in the morgue or a hospital and was hoping you would show me around, help me make my decision.'

He offered me a tour and I followed him down to the morgue.

'Have you seen a dead body before?' the coroner asked before we entered the mortuary fridge.

'Yes Sir, in our second year we were allowed to observe, now that I'm graduating, the professors have encouraged us to find places that need assistance so we can learn more first-hand before we get placed in an intern residency,' I said with an innocent smile.

He returned the smile and I followed him into the room. It was freezing, which was understandable since these rooms had to be kept under 5 degrees.

'I will begin with the basics, an autopsy. You can observe for the first body; with the second body, I will let you assist. Does that sound fair?' he asked. He seemed eager to teach.

I wasn't sure why it seemed like a ghastly one in my opinion.

He picked up the clipboard at the end of the table and cursed under his breath.

'I'm sorry, I must have left her file in the office. I'll just be a moment.'

When he left the room, I pulled the sheet back and groaned. It was the gothic girl. I quickly pulled out a syringe and filled it with her blood. In a rush, I covered her body and ran out of the room, accidently bumping into the coroner.

'Are you alright?' he asked me, concerned.

'Perhaps I'm not as ready as I thought,' I said before continuing down the hall, determined to get out as quickly as possible. I ran home and back up to my room, dropping to all fours on the floor.

I placed the crystal knife in front of me and poured the blood from the coroner's office on to it. Holding my hands over the blade, I whispered an enchantment. Smiling when the crystal started to glow and absorb the blood. I picked up the now dark, coloured blade, feeling safer knowing I'd have this on me.

# CHAPTER TWENTY-FOUR

I lay on my bedroom floor with my feet leaning up against the window, watching the sun go down, the grimoire laying on my chest. I twirled the ring around my finger and willed myself to open the grimoire and read it. I ran the ring over the spine, and it shone blue, activating the book. Opening it I found the entry from the day I lost control of my magic.

*Today I felt had I died inside. My soul had drowned in darkness, the anger and pain erupting a power in me I had never known, a monster inside me so powerful I could barely control it. I stood over an unmarked grave where the coffin had not yet been buried, cut across my palm, letting my blood fall into the grave and I called on the goddess of revenge, claiming the darkness.*

I closed the grimoire and dropped it on the floor beside me. It didn't even matter what it said, I knew who I was. I didn't want to remember the past, and who I had become. My bedroom door opened but I didn't look, I knew it was Raiyn. He threw boxing gloves at me which landed on my stomach. I sat up and glared at him. He was holding the pads and signalled me to come downstairs. I changed into my gym pants and sports top before joining him in the backyard, Raiyn held the pads up for me to hit, so I pulled the gloves on and stood before him stretching.

'Where were you the other night?' he asked as I threw my first punch.

I glared at him, punching again, harder this time. I felt his eyes watching me.

'I went to Jareth,' I said, as I continued punching, letting out all my frustration.

'Is that all?' he asked. 'I can still smell *him* on you.'

I knew who he spoke of. I kept punching, harder and harder. I wasn't ready to answer. I continued punching till Raiyn stepped back, shaking his hand. I must have hit too hard.

'I went to Jareth's. Then afterwards, I went to a motel when *he* found me – I fed from him.'

Raiyn looked at me, horror struck.

'I feel like I don't know you anymore,' he muttered before walking back inside.

I wanted to call him back and explain, but there was no point.

I went back up to my room, picking up the grimoire again before sitting on the bed.

*The pain set in as Jedhail walked away leaving me in the gentle rain, thunder echoing across the sky silencing my screams of anguish. As the magic was dragged to the bottom of my soul so was a part of myself. The magic was a part of me and burying it away took more of me than I had expected. The emptiness was replaced by fear, doubt and regret. I don't know who I am anymore. I look into the mirror and see something I'm ashamed of. I am a legend, nothing more.*

I wasn't a legend, I was me, and I was going to finish this. I grabbed the dead man's blood knife and a set of clothes which I threw in a small pouch which was magically expandable inside. I threw it around my neck and undressed. If our kind ever wanted to transform back to human in a different location we'd have to take clothes with us.

I transformed into my cat form and ran through the forest, when suddenly I stopped in my tracks. I could smell Christopher. I heard him move from his location and I ran towards the direction of his house sensing he was somewhere behind me. But I wasn't quick enough. His nails scratched my back, making me snarl in pain.

I continued running till I could no longer sense him and I transformed back into human form as I reached Christopher's house. My back was wet with blood, he had broken my skin. I didn't want to go inside now that I smelt like blood and knew Christopher wasn't far behind but it was too late to turn around for the safety of home. I needed to find Jedhail. I pulled the clothes from the pouch to change and put the knife safely in my jacket.

I walked to the front door. Raven answered the door after I knocked, stepping out and closing the door behind her.

She confronted me. 'Are you working with my brother?'

'Jedhail?' I questioned. 'Definitely not.'

'Why have anything to do with him then?' Raven interrogated. 'I know he's been with you.'

'BECAUSE HE MURDERED RHYS!' I yelled.

She looked shocked, opening her mouth as though she was going to say something comforting, but changed her mind.

'I killed Elphina - now I am going to kill him. I don't care that he is your brother.'

She sighed and opened the door letting me in. 'This is just vengeance for you, isn't it?' she asked as I walked past her.

I looked at her for a moment before nodding.

'Are you bleeding?' Raven asked as we walked into the back yard.

I ignored her question by asking her my own. 'Do you know where your brother is?'

'Christopher is on his way back from a run,' Echo answered, assuming that's who I was talking about. 'Why do you smell of blood?'

Christopher walked into the yard and I took a step back from him, the memory of his nails on my back making me want to growl at him. Then a cold chill ran down my spine. Raven and I both looked at each other with concern... Jedhail was here.

'Isn't this a nice family reunion?' said Jedhail's sadistic voice, as he walked out of the forest towards us.

Christopher and Jarret bared their fangs in anger. Raven softly whispered his name, a slight air of begging to it.

'You're not welcome here,' Echo hissed.

Jedhail put on a pretend sad face before turning to me. 'I heard you were looking for me. Ready to finish this?' He laughed, looking at his family. 'Have you not told them who you are?'

'What is he talking about?' Christopher asked. I ignored him. 'ARYA!'

I turned to him, seeing anger and confusion on his face. I was about to say I was sorry but realised I had nothing to apologise for. I turned back to Jedhail, a smirk on my face. Above us a storm started to brew. Jedhail pulled out a potion vial from his back pocket, murmuring something about fireworks as he tossed it at me. I threw up a ward, the potion exploding against it and bouncing back almost hitting Jedhail. I grabbed the knife and threw it at his chest. He caught it, the tip of the knife was barely a centimetre from his heart. He laughed nervously as he lowered it realising how close it had been.

'I'll meet you where it all began,' he said.

I threw another spell at him which knocked him off his feet, the force of the hit causing him to drop the knife. I ran over and grabbed the knife, turning to find that Jedhail had disappeared into the forest.

Raiyn suddenly appeared at my side.

'Who the hell is this?' Jarret yelled. 'And what just happened? Can someone please explain?'

'You don't have to do this, Arya,' Raiyn said, ignoring Jarret's questions.

'How did you know where I was?' I yelled, itching to go after Jedhail.

'I sensed your magic,' he said, holding his hand out. 'Take my hand. I can take you away from all this.'

I looked up at him. He had said these words to me before. *I had been really young before I had stopped aging. I'd gotten lost in the forest and I was waiting for Rhys to find me, but Raiyn showed up instead. He'd said those exact words. I'd taken his hand then.*

I took a step back from Raiyn. 'I'm sorry,' I whispered, returning the knife to the safety of my jacket. 'If I lose control again, kill me,' I said before disappearing in a cloud of black smoke.

# CHAPTER TWENTY-FIVE

*'You will regret this; I will make you pay for rejecting me. You're too broken, haunted by those beautiful terrible things you did. Does the screaming still haunt you? How does it feel? Vengeance. Blood.'*

Jedhail's voice echoed in my head as I walked down the street to my old house in Versattali, the house I had left only a few weeks ago. I didn't think I would be back so soon. When I reached the front door I pushed it open. I was surprised to see it looked the same. I knew it would, but it felt like it should have changed, or maybe it was just me that had changed so much. I walked upstairs to Rhys's room, and over to his piano, running my fingers over it, waiting for Jedhail.

'I'm surprised to find you here,' said a voice from the doorway. I didn't need to turn to know it was him.

'You said where it began,' I whispered, knowing he'd hear me. 'This is where you killed him.'

He came up behind me and pushed me to the wall. I kneed him in the groin and threw him across the room with a burst of energy. I threw the knife at him again, but he dodged it. The knife became embedded in the wall. Jedhail was in front of me in a flash of an eye, flinging me across the room into the mirror. The glass shattered all over the floor as I hit the ground. I groaned in pain as I pulled pieces of glass out of my leg and stomach. I stood, leaning against the wall for balance and pulled my knife out of the wall just before he threw me to the floor again.

When I stood up this time, he pinned me against the wall. 'Why don't you fight harder?' he snarled.

'You're not worth it,' I spat.

He sunk his teeth into my neck. I flinched at the pain, but started laughing. I felt him pause in surprise. He pulled away and slapped me across the face. I fell to the floor again, still laughing.

'Why are you so amused when you're on the verge of being killed?' he asked, exasperated.

I pulled out the crystal knife and threw it to him. It was no longer red.

'When you tossed me into the wall, I stabbed myself, injecting the dead man's blood into my system.'

Christopher and Raven suddenly ran into the room. Jedhail's confident demeanour faltered momentarily before he attacked Christopher.

'Are you okay?' I heard Raven ask as she knelt down beside me.

Christopher groaned in agony causing Raven to leave my side and run over to defend one brother and kill the other. I saw Raven pull a silver blade from her jacket and slash across Jedhail's chest. He fell to his knees and hissed at Raven. Grabbing her wrist, he pulled her down to him. Before she could react, Jedhail sunk his teeth into Raven's throat. She screamed out in pain. Christopher pulled Jedhail off Raven and threw him against the wall. I didn't see what happened next because I fell unconscious from blood loss.

*I found myself standing in crystal blue waters under a waterfall. Rhys was walking towards me. I ran out of the water onto the grass and threw myself in Rhys's arms, kissing him passionately.*

*'I love you,' I whispered between kisses.*

*He pulled away. 'I love you too, but it's not your time yet.'*

The memory of the fight flashed across my mind and I woke up to find myself in a hospital bed. I cursed under my breath. You'd think I'd be happy that I hadn't died, especially at the hands of the man I hated most, but I would have been with Rhys. I suddenly noticed I wasn't alone in the room - Echo, Raven and Christopher were standing around me.

'Jedhail is dead,' Raven said, sitting on the side of my bed.

'You should have let me die too,' I said softly.

Christopher looked offended. 'What is wrong with you?' he fumed. 'You almost died and all you can say is we should have let you.'

Raven looked at me, as though she was asking if she needed to step in. I shook my head. He deserved an answer.

'What do you want to hear Christopher, a thank you? Well thank you, for leading Jedhail to my family almost forty years ago. Thank you for him killing the one person I had loved more than life itself. Thank you for him destroying my life every time I tried to rebuild it. So I've been hunting him ever since, not caring if I live or die. So yes, I wish you had let me die, because in those few moments I was dying, I saw Rhys again.'

Christopher looked at me confused. I pulled up my sleeve and showed them my tattoo. I saw all of them begin to realise how they knew me, but then confusion crossed their faces over how they had forgotten.

'According to my grimoire I cast a spell, making us forget each other,' I said, not meeting Christopher's gaze. 'Now that I've revealed myself, we should all remember everything within a few hours.'

Christopher stormed out without another word, Raven running after him. I was surprised to find Echo still standing before me.

'I understand the look now,' she said, taking a step towards me. 'When we first met and you asked about me wanting to be human, you had this look. I thought you were just feeling sorry for me, but you recognised how I felt, didn't you?'

'I don't want my immortality. The person that would make it worthwhile was taken from me.'

'Rhys?' she asked. 'You kept whispering Rhys when you were unconscious and I realised I know you, not from the war, not from your affair with Christopher, but from Rhys.'

'You knew Rhys?' I asked softly.

She nodded. 'I was hunting and came across a black cat. He turned human and pinned me down. I was so shocked; I had no idea what he was. So he told me about his species, then he started talking about this girl he was in love with. He spoke of her eyes, her heart and her soul, so I followed him when he left. I needed to know who this amazing girl was. It was you.'

I didn't know what to say. I'd never known how much I loved him until I'd lost him. I'd always loved him as a brother, but I'd never loved him in the other way. I couldn't because I'd grown up seeing him as my brother, but he wasn't. We weren't related. I looked at Echo, seeing the same yearning for humanity I held within myself.

'Just be grateful you know what it's like to be human,' I muttered.

'Don't we all?' she questioned.

I shook my head. 'No, I was born this way.'

'How is that possible?' she said incredulously.

I shrugged. She smiled sadly at me, giving me a hug before she left. We both knew each other's pains. We both knew we had no choice but to live with it.

Memories of Christopher had started flooding back into my mind.

*I was standing in a ballroom wearing a gorgeous, dark blue, corset dress. I played with the pearl necklaces around my neck. It was a Christmas party. I stood at the back of the party watching the festivities. Before I knew it, someone pulled me into the hallway and kissed me more passionately than I'd ever felt.*

*The kiss ended and I opened my eyes.*

*'You're not Mikhail,' I snapped, feeling guilty.*

*'No I am not,' he said with a temptingly sweet smile. 'I'm Christopher.'*

*'Why did you do that?' I fumed.*

*'Because I wanted to know what it would be like to kiss the most beautiful girl I have ever seen.'*

*I blushed at his compliment. 'I'm already spoken for,' I said, reminding myself also.*

*'And?' he asked, cockiness noticeable in his voice.*

*'And... I don't see myself ending it with him any time soon.'*

*He shrugged, his fingers brushing my lips. 'I have forever on my side,' he said before walking away.*

Raiyn walked into the room as I came out of the memory, carrying a bunch of red roses. I smiled at him.

'The roses are from Lorelei,' he said as he put them on the table and came sat on my bed. 'We've been covering for you from Mum and Dad. They don't know where you went, or are, at the moment.'

'I didn't kill him,' I said, knowing that's what he really wanted to ask.

He hugged me. The last thing I'd said to him was asking him to kill me and he was probably dreading me losing control. He stood up and smiled at me.

'Take my hand. I can take you away,' he said offering me his hand.

I reached forward and took his hand. He held me to him and we vanished in a cloud of black smoke. I opened my eyes and looked around, still holding his hand. I smiled as I recognised the place; this was the place he'd rescued me from when I'd gotten lost.

'I don't want to ever lose you again,' he said, softy. 'Lorelei and I are leaving. We decided we need to spend a year by ourselves, since we never really recovered. None of us have, being in that house, avoiding what happened. You can come see us whenever you want.'

I faked a smile. 'I love you.'

He pulled a folded envelope from his back jeans pocket. I knew it was old because it was yellow and crinkled. He handed it to me.

'It's from Rhys,' he said as I took it. 'He wrote it before you two left for the war.'

We teleported back home and I walked into the backyard holding the letter to my chest. I sat on the grass and opened it slowly.

*Dear Arya, my love.*

*If I don't survive the war I just want you to know that I love you. More than a sister. More than my life. More than this world.*

*You are my heart and my soul.*

*And I want you to leave Mikhail. And end your affair with Christopher. I wanted to tell you this after the war but if you're reading this letter I didn't survive.*

*I want someone to love you more than anything, I want someone to give you more love than a hundred people could. If I was able to, I would show you this love.*

*Promise you won't give up. Don't choose Mikhail. Don't choose Christopher.*

*I love you,*

*Rhys.*

# CHAPTER TWENTY-SIX

It had been a week since I'd left the hospital.

I decided to go to Alesmera. The castle doors were opened as I entered Ariella's domain. I was glad she had won the throne of Alesmera. But I now had to help her on one last task. Plus it kept my mind distracted from what I'd been through the past few weeks.

I walked through the hall up to Ariella who sat on her throne.

'Your Majesty,' Jace and Nancy said in unison whilst bowing.

I handed them both a small box, and smiled at their looks of amazement as they opened them. I'd given them fallen stars. They looked like small glowing crystals. Nancy's transformed into a tiger and Jace's into an otter. Fallen stars took the form of the owner's soul animal.

'Where is she?' I asked Nancy softy, hoping Ariella wasn't listening. 'She isn't with…'

'No,' Jace interrupted, glad I didn't have to finish the sentence. 'I'm returning to her now.'

'It's nice to see you fully dressed,' Ariella said as I turned my attention to her. I handed her a small black box. It contained the locket. The one Jareth had was a fake, I'd stolen it years ago.

'I am here to accompany you so we should get going. It's a long journey to the Unclaimed Lands,' I said, steering the focus away from the locket.

Nancy, Ariella and I headed to Styr's. The journey would take too long without his help.

'What can I do for you ladies?' he asked as he exited his office.

'We need to go into the Unclaimed Lands,' I said with more force than I intended.

'I will not allow it,' Styr said, shaking his head.

'Cut the hippie crap, Styr. We need to enter. It's a rescue mission,' I snapped, rolling my eyes.

He moved to stand right in front of me, his mind searching mine. I wasn't sure what he was hoping to find but he smiled and took a step back.

'Please, I need to save my little sister,' Nancy begged, stepping forward.

*'You told me to get Ariella on the throne,'* I said to Styr telepathically. *'I sent Nancy to help her achieve that in exchange for helping her rescue her kid sister from the Vampires in the Unclaimed Lands. Let us cross.'*

Styr looked from Nancy to me. I could see the battle raging on in his head. He sighed and agreed to let us out on the mountain. He wouldn't cross too far into the Unclaimed Lands.

'You won't like what you find, Arya,' he yelled out to me as we stepped through.

It took us two days to find the Vampires holding Nancy's sister hostage. Nancy opened the front door and I pulled my sword out, ready for an attack. Nancy and Ariella walked up the stairs. As they disappeared from sight, a Vampire jumped at me, but I'd seen him coming. I slashed his head off, watching him fall into dust. I ran up the stairs to find the others but was ambushed by three other Vampires. One threw me into a door. I crashed into the room and was glad to see Nancy, Lydia and Ariella.

I began the attack on every Vampire in our path, giving Nancy a clear path to get Lydia out. I ran down the stairs, still fighting. Then *he* walked into the room, his blonde hair tucked behind his ears, the green eyes I used to love now black.

'I'm surprised to see you, my love,' he said to me.

I felt my heart pounding in my chest as I whispered his name. 'Quinn…'

I could hear Ariella calling me, but I wasn't listening. I couldn't take my eyes off him. How was he still alive? Why was he here?

'I've missed you,' he said with a smirk. 'I missed the fun we used to have.'

Ariella called my name again.

'I'll see you soon, my love,' he said before turning away. I rushed out the door and didn't stop walking until I was near the graveyard.

'Did you kill him?' Nancy asked, pulling me from my racing mind.

'Did you know he was here?' I yelled. He was her brother, or used to be.

I saw her flinch at my rage. 'I had a feeling.'

'What is going on?' Ariella asked. 'Arya, are you okay?'

'No,' I said, my voice breaking under my emotions. 'I didn't kill him. You know I can't,' I said to Nancy before walking away.

I started running till I reached the forest. It was now pouring with rain. I leaned on a tree and sunk down to the ground, my hands to my head, fighting the urge to scream. The rain hid my tears. I heard footsteps approaching. The King of the Dark Elves kneeled before me.

'I'm not in the mood, Allister.'

'I can feel your darkness fighting to the surface,' he said.

'Go away,' I snarled.

He lifted my chin so my eyes met his. 'Are you sure you don't want to be my queen? I promise you if you join me, you'll never have to feel heartbreak again.'

I stayed silent... The promise of no more pain seduced me.

# CHAPTER TWENTY-SEVEN

ONE MONTH LATER

I stood in the shower, in a daze, the hot water stinging my back. I was starting to worry. It had been weeks and Christopher's scratches on my back weren't healing. I got out of the shower, throwing a shirt and underwear on before falling into bed.

I fell asleep in an instant.

I wasn't sure if I was dreaming or not. Everything was so real. The wind was cold against my bare arms and legs, the leaves beneath my feet were damp. This was too vivid to be a dream, but I remembered falling asleep.

I started walking through the dark forest, the moonlight sneaking through the trees. I felt something unnatural and sinister up ahead. I continued towards it. Each step was silent as I ducked under low branches and stepped only on the wet leaves.

In the back of my mind I could hear my name, as though someone was trying to wake me up. Though I continued walking in the direction I was going, losing all sense of control, there was something up ahead that my mind wanted me to see.

Peering through the trees I saw two men in hooded cloaks. It looked like they were performing a ritual. They were chanting in an old language that I wasn't fluent in, though from the few words I picked up it sounded like they were trying to resurrect a demon. One of the men pulled his hood back, revealing his face. I gasped. It was Aaron Malcolm. I'd wondered what had happened to Jedhail's human. It seemed he was seeking a new master.

Frowning, I took a step forward but was suddenly thrown back by an enormous, green blast of light. I closed my eyes from where I lay in the dirt. As the light dimmed I opened my eyes and groaned at who I saw.

Elphina.

Jedhail was finally gone and someone brings back his psychotic girlfriend. Her black eyes found Aaron. She rushed over to him and sunk her teeth into his neck. I supposed being dead for over thirty years would make you hungry.

I stood up, accidently stepping on a stick. It cracked loudly. Elphina dropped Aaron's body and locked eyes on me. I'd prepared myself to teleport, but I wasn't quick enough. As I vanished into black smoke I felt her electric webs wrap around me.

I screamed as I reappeared in a room, hitting the floor, winding me. I managed to open my eyes for a second to find myself in Christopher's room rather than my own. I dissolved into the black smoke again and fell onto the floor of Christopher's living room. I screamed as the webs cut deeper into my skin, the electricity shocking my whole body. Echo was the first to my side, cutting the webs off and throwing them away. I coughed up blood that I'd swallowed from my bleeding lip as I tried to catch my breath. The cuts on my arms from the webs were not healing.

Christopher was suddenly leaning over me, his storm grey eyes filled with fear. He began wrapping my wounds as I caught my breath.

'What happened?' Raven asked from behind Christopher.

'Elphina,' I coughed, 'is back.'

Echo came and leant down beside me again. 'She did this to you? I thought you were stronger than her? I mean, weren't you the one to kill her?'

'When I killed her I was consumed with dark magic,' I said with frustration. 'Plus I didn't know she was actually being resurrected. I was dreaming.'

Echo placed her hand on my back and I winced in pain. She noticed and pulled the back of my shirt up. Christopher paled when he saw the claw marks down my back. He must have worked out it was him that did it.

'These aren't from her. Why aren't you healing?' Christopher exclaimed.

'Don't like your handy work?' I snapped rudely back. He winced.

Echo cut her hand and let a few drops of blood fall into the claw marks. My eyes turned black, the scent of her blood entering my nose. I disappeared into the smoke again, and out of that house. The animal inside me growled and its mind took over. I snarled, searching for more blood.

I smelled alcohol up ahead. Walking through the alley I found the back door to a bar, a man stumbling out of it. He looked at me hungrily, walking up to me and tried to smirk at me as though he was god's gift. I smiled back at him before pinning him up against the wall, the scent of his desire filled my nose arousing me more. I sank my teeth into him, feeling his heartbeat start to slow as I drained the life from him.

Something pulled me off him and threw me into the wall. I looked up to see Styr standing over my victim, checking his pulse. As he walked over to me I growled, but he tapped his fingers to my forehead and I became immobilised. I tried to scream but my mouth wouldn't move. I growled inside my head at Styr. He closed my eyes and picked me up.

I felt him put me on something soft before he took the spell off me. I opened my eyes to find myself on my own bed, groaning at my pounding headache. What had happened?

I turned to see Styr sitting by my bed, looking at me with concern. I groaned again. Elphina was back, and

I almost killed a man. I winced as Styr put some kind of ointment in the scratches on my back. He had me sit up so he could unbandage my arms, cleaning my wounds.

'Kill me,' I whispered.

Styr looked up to meet my gaze. He put the bandages on the bed beside me and placed his hands on either side of my face.

'You listen to me,' he said firmly. 'I've lived for hundreds of years, watched millions of people, and none are as amazing as you. I've seen your worst and your best and you are still the most exquisite creature I've ever come across. I need you to stay strong and beat this – you need to reveal your colours within. Stop hiding your true self.'

I leaned forward into his arms and he hugged me. There was a knock on the door so I sat back and saw Christopher standing in the doorway. Styr continued to clean the cuts in my arms.

'We're leaving,' he said. I looked at him shocked.

'But why?' I started to ask before it clicked. 'Elphina. I can help.'

He shook his head.

'You have no idea who you are dealing with,' I spat angrily.

'They are MY FAMILY!' he shouted. 'You've done enough.'

I went to argue, but Styr put his hands in mine. I looked away from Christopher and at Styr.

'You can't fight her again, my love,' he said gently. 'Remember what happened last time? Vila is still a ghost town from what happened.'

'That was you?' Christopher interrupted. I looked at him quick enough to see a look of disgust and horror cross his face.

*He thought I was a monster. But he helped make me this way. I won't apologise for the monster I became when no one has said they are sorry for making me this way.*

I snatched my hand from Styr's and excused myself. I got up and ran out of the room. As I ran down the stairs and out of the house I asked myself, *How do you stop the monsters without becoming one yourself?*

I kept running, not stopping until I was on the cliff edge where I'd bargained for Lorna's life.

# CHAPTER TWENTY-EIGHT

It'd been weeks since Christopher and his family had left. I sat on the bar top in the bar that Lorna worked at, leaning against the wall, with my nose in a book. It was an unnaturally dark night out, mist rolling in every time the door opened. Even when the door was closed you could hear the thunder.

I looked up from my book and saw only a handful of customers left in the venue. A handsome guy with blonde shoulder-length hair sat at the bar. I watched Lorna clean the dirty glasses. It must be the end of her shift soon.

I put my attention back in my book when I felt a cold breeze blow into the bar. I pretended that I didn't notice but my eyes looked up from my book. I watched a man with black, slicked back hair walk to the bar and sit in front of Lorna.

'What can I get you?' she asked. I heard a change in her voice - she sensed his darkness also. His skin was extremely pale, his black eyes looking her over.

'Aren't you the sweetest thing,' he said, leaning across the bar.

I growled, lowering my book. His eyes met mine and he smiled seductively. It reminded me of Jedhail's. He had the same over-confident charisma.

'Red wine,' he said, turning back to Lorna.

After serving the man Lorna went out back to change because her shift was finally over. The stranger looked over at me. He drank the wine before walking out. What shocked me was the blonde followed him.

'You know you don't have to chill out at the bar with me on all my shifts,' Lorna said as we walked home. Lorna was now living in Raiyn and Lorelei's room, since they'd left. I shrugged and held up my book.

We turned the corner into the street and both paused for a second. There weren't any lights on - it was pitch black. The mist swirling around the roads made it feel like a horror movie in the making. We walked down the street, my senses on high alert.

When we got inside I tried to turn the lights on to find them not working.

'Blackout,' Lorna said logically. 'I'm off to bed. Night.'

I watched her walk upstairs. I knew I was being paranoid but I checked the house. The storm hadn't been so bad that it would cause a blackout. I walked upstairs to my room and sat before my bathroom mirror, the scars on my arms still healing, very slowly.

'We never got a chance to talk back there,' said an amused voice.

I jumped. The man from the bar was standing in the doorway to my bathroom. I stood up, wishing I'd kept weapons in my bathroom. I put a magical shield up before me, keeping him at a distance.

He laughed. 'I'm Ashard,' he said offering a hand, knowing I wouldn't take it. 'I'm looking for Christopher.'

'He's not here,' I snapped.

He offered me a vial. 'I want you to drink this.'

I shook my head, making sure my shield was still strong.

He sighed. 'We could do this the easy way, or the hard way. Now my better half is in the other room with Lorna, waiting to tear out her throat, so either drink this or your best friend is dead.'

I let my senses roam and felt the presence of another Vampire in Lorna's room.

'What is it?' I asked, as I lowered my shield and took the vial from his hand.

'Power.'

I looked at the vial suspiciously.

'Lorna is running out of time,' he snapped, impatiently.

Exhaling my nerves, I swallowed the contents in one sip. The moment it passed my lips I felt sick and my head started to pound. I cried out in pain, falling to my hands and knees.

'It's Elphina's blood mixed with dark magic,' Ashard explained. 'She wants you back to how you were in Vila.'

I teleported into the street, trying to cough up the liquid as well as getting as far away as I could from Ashard. I looked up and saw the blonde from the bar walking towards me. I growled at him as he neared me and attacked. I lunged at him, slashing my claws at him, but he threw me back like I was nothing. Landing elbow first on the gravel, I groaned in agony.

Ashard suddenly appeared before me as someone grabbed me from behind. I felt nails on my neck and knew it was Elphina holding me. She let her electric webs free to wrap their way around my neck, and arms. I felt my old wounds reopening.

*"Raiyn"*, my mind cried out as the webs burnt my neck, forgetting momentarily that he didn't live here anymore.

Ashard was pulled away from me by the blonde. Elphina's web tightened around my neck, causing me to cry out in pain. Both Ashard and the blonde looked at me. Elphina clicked her tongue against her teeth in annoyance. I was twitching in pain, suppressing my cries as the web's electricity burnt my skin.

'Now boys,' Elphina said in a girly voice. 'Didn't your mamma tell you that girls don't like fighting?'

Ashard walked over to us, grabbing me from Elphina's grasp. Her webs remained around my neck and arms. Elphina smiled sweetly at Ashard before walking towards the blonde.

'What is your business here, Vampire?' she asked.

He snarled at her and slashed at her. Ashard and I got behind her.

Ashard sunk his teeth into my neck, and I cried out, closing my eyes from the pain. When he released me and I opened my eyes Elphina was gone.

'Let go of my sister!' I heard someone yell.

Ashard was pulled off me and I fell to the ground. I let out of a cry of relief when I saw Raiyn's face. He tore the webs off me and I threw my arms around his neck. Behind Raiyn I saw the blonde walking off, Ashard's body lay on the road.

# CHAPTER TWENTY-NINE

The next morning I woke up alone, though I remembered Raiyn falling asleep next to me. He must have left earlier in the morning to return to Lorelei. I put my hand to my neck and winced, it was still red raw. What was wrong with my healing abilities lately?

I walked into the bathroom, stripping off my pyjama shirt. Looking over my reflection I sighed. I had burn and cut marks all up my arms and around my neck, all which looked on the verge of bleeding. I turned to look at the scratch marks down my back to see they had reopened. And then there was the new bite mark on my neck. I jumped in the shower, wishing the water could wash off all my injuries.

I suddenly felt a presence. Walking out of the shower, I wrapped my body in a towel. I went to my window and looked into the street. The blonde stood at the end watching my house. When he saw me he turned and walked away. I threw on shorts and a singlet before running down stairs and out of the house. When I got to the end of the street, I noticed his scent went into the forest.

I transformed into my cat form and dashed through the forest, following his scent. If anyone was in the forest, they'd see a large black cat wearing shorts. Luckily my singlet was the same colour as my fur so at least it blended in a little bit. As his scent got stronger I slowed. I saw him through the trees. He paused and looked around as I came into his line of sight, he looked at me and went to walk away. I transformed back into my human form, adjusting my now stretched loose clothes.

'You don't smell like a Nagual,' he said bluntly.

'You don't exactly smell like a normal Vampire either,' I said back. 'Why were you at my house?'

He shrugged and kept walking.

I followed him. We came out of the forest into a cul-de-sac. Only one house occupied the street. I kept following him till he reached the front door.

'Well, since you followed me home, do you want to come in so I can check your wounds?' he asked after opening the door. 'Ethan Deandray,' he said, before walking inside, leaving the door open for me.

*Deandray? As in the original Knight of the Animas Tenebris?*

*The original Deandray Vampire was legendary. He was sired at the Animas Tenebris power base by one of the head*

*Vampires. He became a knight, protector figure for them until he decided to go solo.*

Even if he wasn't, curiosity got the better of me and I followed him inside. The house was denied light, the walls were oak. I closed the door behind me and walked into the living room; all the furniture was black.

'Are you...' I started to ask.

'Nope, that would be my older brother Tyler you are thinking of,' he said cutting me off. He must've known what I was going to ask.

I never knew there was a brother.

He signalled me to sit so I sat on one of the single chairs. He came over to me holding a damp cloth and a bottle of ointment. I didn't recognise the liquid by sight or smell. He put some of the ointment on the cloth before rubbing it down my arms. I winced at the contact, it stung like a bitch. He then wiped my neck, hesitating over the bite mark.

'Why aren't you healing yourself?' he asked.

I looked up into his eyes, his face was so close to mine. His eyes reminded me of Mikhail's. He was looking at me the same way Mikhail always had. I looked at his lips, then leaned forward and kissed him. He pulled away from me and for a moment I felt awkward over what I'd just done.

He leaned in so his lips were almost touching mine, I kissed him again. I felt the movements of his arms as he put the cloth and ointment down on the bench beside me, wrapping his arms around me as the kiss continued.

For some reason my mind went to the last conversation I'd had with Christopher: *"They are my family!"* his voice yelled in my head.

I pushed Ethan off me.

'She's punishing Jedhail for failing,' I whispered to myself. 'She knew they would be harder to persuade to her side. She could have taken an easier victim but she's punishing him for failing. She's going to kill them. She is going to kill Jedhail's whole family in the end.'

I muttered sorry and thanks to Ethan before running out of his house.

# CHAPTER THIRTY

I sat on the cliff, my legs hanging over the lake down below.

What game was Elphina playing? She turned Ashard and Laney, turned them into her slaves just like she did to Jedhail, which forced the rest of the family's hand, making them kill their own. That's her revenge on Jedhail. But what about me? She didn't believe I was strong enough anymore. She wanted to unleash the monster inside me.

A twig snapped behind me. I sat up straight and turned around but it was just Ethan. I turned back away from him. He came and sat beside me, letting his feet hang as well.

'Do you want to explain to me why a Spider Demon is coming after you and punishing this Jedhail character?' he asked.

'Because I killed her first,' I said, not looking at him. 'Jedhail was meant to kill me for her, but I killed Elphina, then allowed his family to kill him.'

'Why'd you kiss me?' he asked, completely changing the subject.

'It seemed like a good idea at the time,' I said with a shrug.

He brushed his fingers along my chin, making me turn to look at him. He leant in and kissed me so I kissed him back, sinking into the passion.

'This probably isn't a good thing to do on the edge of a cliff,' I pointed out, pulling away.

He smiled at me. 'It's obvious you enjoy your immortality with your call list of infatuations, but do you actually love any of them?'

I scoffed, standing up. He stood up beside me.

*"I'm not implying anything,"* he said within my mind.

'I have the ability to read minds, and the other day when you were at the bar, I heard you think about Mikhail, Rhys, Christopher and Quinn.' I looked at him as he said the last name. 'Do you love any of them?'

'Rhys was like my brother, so I loved him, but I was never with him to know if I was in love with him. Mikhail was my fiancé so I must have felt something real, but then I cheated on him with Christopher,' I explained.

'What about Quinn?'

My eyes met his. 'I could have loved him, but Jedhail turned him.'

'Who would you choose if you could?'

'None,' I said.

He understood by my tone that I didn't want to elaborate. He shook his head as he went to walk away, but I grabbed his hand, pulling him into a kiss. He pulled me closer and kissed me passionately.

'I should go,' I said softly breaking free. 'I told Lorna I'd meet her and the guys after school.'

'Will you come to mine tonight?' he asked. 'I'll help you get rid of Elphina again.'

I nodded and smiled before walking off.

***

As I entered the school zone, I saw Matthew, Kirstin and Logan sitting with Lorna at one of the tables. I approached them and took a seat on the table facing Logan.

'Whose heart are you breaking this weekend?' I asked.

He faked a laugh, 'Says the queen of heart breakers.' I rolled my eyes. 'I actually have a weekend in with my bro,' he said, throwing a ball of paper at Matthew.

'Are you even enrolled here anymore?' Matthew asked me. 'I'm pretty sure you've missed more days than you're meant to.'

I shrugged.

'Yeah, you need to start showing up more or Lorna will be the only girl,' Logan said.

Missy's parents had moved towns a few weeks ago and Kirstin was dropping out. Today was her last day.

Kirstin checked her watch. She was waiting for her lift.

Lorna pulled out her textbook and started highlighting notes as Matthew and Logan went back to their conversation. I lay across the table, leaning into Lorna's textbook.

'Are you working this weekend?' I asked.

She nodded.

'Where'd you go this morning?' she asked softly, not looking up at me.

'Ethan Deandray's house,' I muttered under my breath.

She slammed the book shut and gave me the *give-me-an-explanation-now* look. I smiled nervously and looked over at the boys who were still in deep conversation.

Her dark brown eyes glared at me from behind her brunette curls. It was time to tell her the truth, since I hadn't even told her about Elphina being back.

'Remember the other night at your work when that blonde guy was at the bar; the night that creepy guy came in?'

She nodded.

'That blonde guy is Ethan, and that night after we got home that creepy guy attacked me. His name is Ashard and he's in league with Elphina.'

'But you killed Elphina a lifetime ago, so how's that possible?'

I glanced quickly at the boys to make sure they weren't eavesdropping. 'She was resurrected.'

Lorna hit me over the head with her book, getting up and dragging me off with her. I yelled a goodbye to the boys over my shoulder.

'Why didn't you tell me?' she said furiously once we were out of hearing range.

I shrugged. 'I wasn't planning to do anything and she hadn't exactly come after me till the other night.'

A motorbike pulled up to the curb and Kirstin hugged the guys, shouting her goodbyes to us before she walked over to the bike. When the rider took off his helmet and brushed back his blonde hair, my heart began to race nervously.

It was Daniel Woodsen. The hunter I'd met at the hotel. He looked very different out of the suit but it was definitely him. As Kirstin got on the motorbike she pulled her shirt collar down and revealed her own Wyatt Hunter tattoo, winking at me as they drove off.

'We have to tell your father,' Lorna said, grabbing my wrist once they were out of sight.

'No, he doesn't need to know,' I said firmly. 'Besides, Wyatts don't kill without proof their prey is guilty.'

'So we're safe?' Lorna asked, visibly relaxing.

'You are,' I muttered.

'What does that mean?'

'It means the hunt is on,' I said, picking up my bag, signalling we should leave.

As we walked home Lorna turned to me and asked, 'Are you interested in Ethan or did you only accept his help in hopes of meeting Tyler?'

'I don't know. You know my heart is complicated.'

Lorna laughed. 'Complicated is an understatement. I think the last person you loved was Quinn and that was years ago.'

'I saw him,' I whispered, not meeting her eyes.

She stopped me in my tracks. 'Quinn? When did you see him?'

'In the Unclaimed Lands. It was the first time I'd seen him since he was turned – his eyes weren't his.'

'Does he know…?'

'No,' I said cutting Lorna off. 'Do you think you could put a protection charm around the house?' I asked, changing the subject.

# CHAPTER THIRTY-ONE

Lorna was serving a customer while I sat on the bar with a book.

'You know we have seats in here,' she said as she wiped down the bar around me.

I smiled at her but continued reading. Though my mind wasn't really reading the book. I was wondering how Aurora's wedding planning was going. Would she go the mortal white gown or the traditional Alesmera, golden, fairy-made dress? And how was Ariella going? Was she having fun ruling Alesmera while spending her nights with Hale? They made a cute couple. I wondered if they'd last. Then there was Jareth. Where did Ariella send him? Was he still alive?

'You look deep in thought,' said a voice.

I put the book down and smiled at Ethan.

'When did you get here?' I asked, as I jumped off the bar and gave him a hug.

'Just then. Your mind was very far away but,' he replied.

I turned to Lorna and introduced them. As we turned to leave she mouthed, *"he's cute"* to me. I rolled my eyes but smiled.

I paused as I stepped outside to see Elphina standing before me.

'Arya, honey!' she said in a mockingly sweet voice. 'Christopher isn't going to be very happy with you, killing his oldest brother. But wait, he doesn't know, because he's still in Illyragasia looking for him.'

In anger I threw a green ball of flame at her which pushed her back. She landed on her back in the dirt, laughing, a cold echoing sound. She stood up and brushed herself off.

'You can do better than that,' she said with a wink before disappearing into the night.

Ethan grabbed hold of me, to keep me from running after her. He led me to his house.

'You can't let her get a rise out of you,' Ethan said as we walked into the lounge room. He sat down with a bunch of folders.

I sat on the couch beside him and he showed me the files he had gathered on her. It was of all her activity, both recent and from before I had killed her. I found a sketch of me standing over her body with a knife. I also found a sketch of her fighting Mikhail.

'How did you get these?' I asked, holding the sketch involving me and Mikhail.

'I've been tracking her for a long time.'

'Why?' I asked, still staring at the sketches.

'She killed the girl I was going to marry,' he said, handing me a small, framed painting.

It was of a blonde, pixie girl with purple eyes. She wore a pink gown, and was magically growing flowers, from her hands.

'A Vampire and a Fairy,' I whispered, handing back the painting. 'That doesn't happen often.'

I pointed to the sketch of Mikhail. 'I was engaged to him when she killed him. That's why I killed her.'

He looked at me, his eyes full of the same sadness that I felt within me. I leaned forward and kissed him. He pulled me into him and kissed me back, full of passion and a need to forget, to move on. In that moment I forgot about Mikhail, Rhys, Quinn, my enemies and even *her*.

***

Ethan and I lay on the couch, wrapped in each other's arms. I propped myself up on his chest, my chin on my hands.

'What is the age difference between you and Tyler?' I asked.

'Hmm, just over a hundred years,' he said after calculating.

'How are you brothers then?' I asked.

'We were both from the same human family line, a few generations apart, of course. I was the last of his human line so he asked the Vampire that sired him to also sire me. So we are brothers in the Vampire sense and blood family in the human sense. Tell me what you know about Elphina,' he asked.

'I met her just before the war started. Jedhail, the vampire she'd convinced to give up his soul, had approached me to join their side. When I turned them down I became their main target.'

'That war was catastrophic. I'm glad the locket became lost with Elphina being back,' he said, more to himself.

'What do you mean?' I asked, having no idea how the locket had anything to do with it, if he was talking about the same locket I was thinking about.

'Didn't you ever wonder how they had such high numbers when the majority of the five kingdoms fought on the same side?'

I'd never actually thought about it, but I nodded to Ethan.

'Elphina used the locket to unleash a prophecy. She opened the mountains so everyone in the Unclaimed Lands could come and fight by her side.'

With a sigh, I ran my fingers through my hair. If Elphina knew how to use the locket she could be the one to unleash the final battle of Azriel. The battle I'd avoided my throne to derail.

'The locket isn't lost,' I told him.

He looked at me with curiosity.

'I've had it for years. I stole it off Aubrey, the King of Alesmera. He must have stolen it off Elphina,' I explained.

'What do you mean had?'

'It's safe,' I assured him. 'There's a prophecy in there, about the five kingdoms aligning with Queens. If the prophecy could be avoided, I would probably claim my throne.'

'The rise of purgatory is an actual prophecy then?' he enquired.

I nodded.

We fell asleep on the couch and I fell into a dream. It started in a shadowed room. *You can't avoid the prophecy forever,* a voice whispered to me.

I closed my eyes and kept whispering to myself, 'I will not be claimed by darkness.'

When I opened my eyes again I was on the cliff in the forest where I'd summoned Hecate. I turned and saw a beautiful pale figure with jet black hair playing across her face in the wind. Her tunnel-like eyes looked straight through me. I started towards her. She turned and ran.

The minute she disappeared out of sight a high-pitched scream pierced the air. I woke up to find myself on the couch alone. I scanned the house for his sense; he must have gone out. I walked to the window and watched the colours of the sunrise bleed through the sky.

# CHAPTER THIRTY-TWO

Lorna had sent me a fire message saying work was boring, so I was walking the streets to the bar. It was a dark and eerie night. Lightning flashed across the sky but no rain fell. Suddenly someone pulled me off the path and down an alley. I kneed the person in the gut and he grunted in pain. I realised then it was Ethan.

'I'm so sorry,' I whispered, my hands over my mouth.

He waved it off, but put a hand to my mouth and a finger to his lips, silencing me.

*Elphina,* he mouthed to me.

I went to ask a question but all of a sudden, I screamed and crouched down in pain as I watched and felt the murders of women, men, children, Fairies and every creature Elphina had ever killed. I saw the pink Fairy from the painting Ethan had showed me. She'd tied her to a tree and tortured her before killing her. I didn't want to see anymore so I retreated into my own mind and trapped myself there.

Walking through my memories I found the day I'd met Quinn. I was high up in a tree, stalking Jedhail.

He was further downstream, but because of the height I was at and the water flowing towards me and not against me, he wouldn't be able to catch my scent. I had my arrow in the bow aimed at his heart. As I went to remove my finger from the string, a voice behind me asked what I was doing. I let out a small squeal of fright and fell from my branch and landed in the steam. I pushed my now wet hair back off my face and glared at the culprit, on the bank, laughing at me. His laugh was so infectious that I couldn't help but smile. He waded into the stream and helped me to my feet. That's when I had noticed his green eyes. He took me back to his home to borrow some of his clothes until mine dried.

I smiled at the memory and walked onto the next one.

It was Rhys and I playing in a field, but the memory wasn't right. Lorna hadn't been there that day, but she stood before me now.

'You need to wake up,' she urged.

'Are you in my head?' I asked.

She nodded, 'I did a spell to enter your mind. It was the only way to talk to you.'

The memory changed around us. We now stood in the Elf village where my grandparents lived. I looked around and saw a young Elf girl, around the age of three running around. She fell over and scraped her hands but she didn't cry, she just dusted her hands off on her dress and jumped back to her feet.

Lorna slapped me, causing the memory to fade around us.

'You need to snap out of this.'

I screamed within my head, willing myself to escape my own mind.

I woke up on the floor. I looked around and saw Ethan and Lorna standing over me. It looked like I was in Lorna's room. Ethan was telling Lorna about what he'd witnessed tonight but he didn't know what Elphina had done to me. Lorna looked down and suddenly noticed I was awake. She knelt down beside me, helping me sit up. Every inch of my body was aching.

Ethan and Lorna both helped me up to my feet.

'What happened?' Lorna asked me, as I found my balance.

'She made me feel and see every person she has ever killed,' I said softly.

I felt Ethan tense beside me. 'Did you see?' he started to ask, unable to finish the question. 'Did she suffer?'

'No,' I lied, shaking my head. 'She had a quick death. Ethan, do you mind if I talk to Lorna alone?'

He shook his head and I offered to walk him out. We walked him to the door but when I opened it I heard someone laugh and a green flame erupted around the house, except for a small gap in which Elphina stood smirking at me.

I pulled myself from Lorna's grasp and ran after Elphina, through the flame. I heard Ethan and Lorna yelling for me to stop but I kept running until I reached a stream. Elphina was gone.

'What do you want?' I yelled, my voice echoing through the forest.

I heard someone behind me. I turned and threw a blue flame at her. She ducked and ran off into the forest again. She was heading to the cliff. I could get there faster. Running through the forest, I went a different way to which she had run but I knew she was going to the cliff and I knew this forest better. I reached the cliff and found I was alone.

I turned around and saw the girl I'd dreamt about the other night.

'Who are you?' I asked taking a small step towards her.

'You don't remember?' she replied, in the voice of an innocent child.

I shook my head. She looked familiar but I couldn't place her. She smiled at my frustration at not knowing who she was. I was also annoyed that Elphina hadn't shown up yet.

She laughed in a childish giggle. 'I'm Laney.'

Oh, that wasn't good. I was in trouble.

'Christopher's sister, right?' I asked, as I took a step back, my eyes searching for a clear path to run.

'I was looking for Ashard,' she said sweetly. 'You don't know where he is, do you?'

That's when I noticed a drawing on her wrist. You could tell it had just been drawn on with a pen, but I wanted to know what it was. I took a step closer to her, hoping to get a better look. It was a drawing of the locket. Elphina must have thought I had it.

Laney turned and ran into the forest as I took another step towards her. Like the dream I heard a piercing cry. I ran in the direction of the scream. I stopped as I saw her standing there, draining the blood from a young girl, but that wasn't the reason I didn't run forward to stop her. Across from me stood Echo and Jarret.

They had also stopped in their tracks when they'd seen me. I stood there in shorts and a singlet while they looked ready to go into battle. When the moment of shock was over, our attention drew back to the issue at hand. Echo ran forward and snapped Laney's neck then drove a stake through her chest for safety measures, while Jarret ran forward and picked up the girl and took off with her. I turned away, not needing to see this. I turned back to Echo as Jarret returned. He walked over and hugged me.

'What are you doing here?' Echo asked as Jarret released me.

'Elphina led me here. I was chasing her.'

Jarret grabbed Echo's hand. 'We need to find Ashard. Stay safe Arya.'

When he said this I froze and looked away from him. I bit my lip wondering what I should say. *Hey, I'm sorry but your brother is dead because he attacked me a few nights ago,* didn't have the right ring to it.

'What?' Echo asked, confused at my reaction.

'He's dead,' I said, uncertain of how they'd react. 'He came after me and got himself killed by another Vampire who is also hunting Elphina.'

We heard movement in the trees. Echo signalled us to move so we walked to the cliff edge to continue the conversation.

'Why did Ashard come after you?' Jarret asked.

'He forced me to drink Elphina's blood,' I told them. 'She wants me to be consumed by dark magic again, so she can beat me at my strongest. It seems she wants a challenge.'

Elphina suddenly appeared before us. When she saw Echo and Jarret her smile faltered for a moment.

'Well, I didn't expect this,' she said in a cheery tone. 'How about this? I'll leave town, stop destroying your family and killing people in your town under one condition.'

'What's the condition?' Echo asked.

Elphina pointed to me. 'She gives me a fight, a challenge.'

I laughed. 'You get what you see,' I said.

'Shame,' she muttered before throwing out her hands. Her electric webs wrapped around me and the force of them threw me back off the cliff. I was falling too fast to scream. I heard Echo screaming my name as I crashed and sunk into the water below.

# CHAPTER THIRTY-THREE

I was dreaming, falling through a vortex. I felt cold water rushing against my skin before I landed on a hard surface. A cruel voice echoed above me.

'It's nice to see you again Arya,' the voice purred. 'Didn't you like my gift in Vila? Why did you give me up?'

'I don't want the darkness,' I whispered.

'Come play with me,' the voice echoed around me.

I closed my eyes, thinking of happy memories. I thought of Raiyn finding me with the roses, I thought about Rhys holding me at night, I thought about *her*.

'Leave me alone,' I shouted. 'I don't want the darkness.'

I woke up coughing. My eyes saw only shadows at first from the sun being so bright above me. I was laying on the hot, rocky ground, my skin starting to burn. *How'd I make it out of the water?* That's when I noticed the girl beside me. She was pale with white blonde hair. Her emerald green eyes watched me closely, her hand on my heart. I coughed up some more water before sitting up.

'I'm Adestria,' the girl said, offering her hand.

*The goddess from Mycenae.*

With a smile of gratitude I took her hand and introduced myself to her.

'I know who you are,' she said. 'I foresaw this and had to come save you.'

'You couldn't have stopped me going off the cliff?' I suggested.

She shrugged apologetically. Beside her I saw a small knife and the remains of Elphina's webs she must have pulled off me. I looked up the cliff and wondered what happened up there, if Echo and Jarret finished off Elphina or if she was still out there.

Adestria helped me to my feet. I swayed slightly on the spot. She let me hold onto her until I got my balance. We heard footsteps ahead and saw Raven and Lorna running towards us. I felt Adestria tense beside me.

Lorna threw her arms around me as she reached us, making me stumble on the spot. Raven smiled and gave me a small side hug, but I could tell her smile was forced.

Adestria bid me farewell and disappeared in a flash of lightning.

'I was told you'd died,' Lorna gasped. 'Raven said that Echo saw you go over the cliff.'

'I did,' I said. I looked at Raven who looked tense. 'What's wrong, Raven?'

'It's Christopher,' she whispered. 'After Echo told us was happened he left for Illyragasia.'

'You don't mean the home of the Animas Tenebris, do you?' Lorna asked.

'Why did he go there?' I asked, before Raven could answer Lorna.

'He's going to ask them to reverse time, to before Jedhail got turned.'

'No!' I shouted. 'We have to go,' I urged, grabbing Raven's wrist.

She pulled herself free. 'I'm not going with you.'

'You need the blood of Nagual, Witch and Vampire to enter the place,' I explained.

'Arya, you're not strong enough. You can barely walk,' Lorna urged.

*Blood.* Before I could ask, Raven offered me her wrist, I looked at her as though asking if she was sure. She nodded. I took her wrist, my feline teeth coming down. The creature in me purred as I sunk my teeth into her wrist and drank her blood. I only took a few mouthfuls, I just needed a small power boost. Plus, I couldn't make Raven weak if she was coming with me. I wiped my mouth and offered Raven thanks.

'Lorna, can you teleport us to the entrance?' I asked. 'I'm still not at full strength.'

Raven and I held hands, and held out our free hands to Lorna who took them after a few seconds of hesitation. I closed my eyes as I felt the air tighten around me. Witch teleportation was a little different to Nagual teleportation. It felt like the air around you was trying to shrink you to fit among its particles. It wasn't very pleasant. I opened my eyes when I felt my feet connect to the ground again. We stood at the entrance of a small, green hedge maze. At the very entrance of the maze was a stone basin. I walked up to the basin and saw little stone statues of a Vampire, a Witch and a Nagual.

I held my hand out to Lorna for a knife. She pulled one out of her bag and handed it to me. Cutting across my palm I let the blood fall on the stone figure of the Nagual. I handed the knife to Lorna, and then to Raven who both followed suit.

The blood absorbed into the stone, and within the maze a red line appeared, showing us the correct directions to the headquarters.

Animas Tenebris was created hundreds of years before, though they only became the ruling system fifty odd years ago. There were three Vampires - Euan, Tristan and Orlando - the oldest living Vampires that anyone knew of. There were two Witches, Carlotta and Adeline, as well as being older than anyone knew, they were the only witches that could play in white and dark magic without consequences. And then there was the Nagual couple, Ruby and Samuel. As far as my kind knew, they were the first - the creators.

We followed the red line all the way to the front door. The building was built with white stone that had aged so much it had turned grey. It looked like a cathedral. A nervous wave suddenly washed over me. It all felt way too easy, but then I understood. I could sense the power from the creatures inside. They knew if someone entered the maze and no-one would be stupid enough to fight against them. Thunder echoed above us. We may have been too late.

I burst through the doors and ran down the hall. When I reached the centre, I noticed it was a crossroads. Sensing the powers, I knew to the left was the Nagual.

'We go this way,' Raven said, running straight.

I broke into a run again, catching up to her. I quickly passed her and burst into the room at the end of the hall, Lorna and Raven running in behind me. We all paused for a second, overwhelmed by the power coming from the three Vampires sitting at the front of the room. They all looked at us, but my eyes were on Christopher who had turned around and looked beyond surprised when he saw me standing there.

# CHAPTER THIRTY-FOUR

I walked forward, feeling the other two keep in step with me, stopping only when we were a few steps ahead of Christopher. I flicked my hair back from my face and stared down the oldest, most powerful Vampires of my time. My senses quickly scanned the room, picking up no major threat, other than the three big ones before me.

'Arya Faith De-Valentino,' said the Vampire that sat centre of the three before me. He was dressed in a long black coat. His grey eyes buried in the purple shadows around them. His black shoulder length hair looked like it'd been gelled down straight and sleek.

'That's me,' I said, holding the tone. 'Who are you?'

'Euan,' he said, a little put off that I didn't know who he was. 'This is Tristan,' he said, waving his hand at the brunette, Prince Charming to his right, 'and Orlando.' He motioned to the blonde punk rocker to his left.

'Pleasure,' I said through my teeth.

'We were made to believe you were dead,' Orlando said coldly, glaring at Christopher behind me.

'Don't be upset by the confusion, even I thought I was dead,' I said sarcastically.

'Arya?' Christopher's voice said from behind me, his voice sounded hoarse. 'Echo and Jarret said…'

'They told you the truth,' I said, not taking my eyes from Euan who kept looking me over. 'Elphina threw me off that cliff and once I stop you from doing this, I'll go find her and she'll get what's coming to her. Oh, and Ashard and Laney are dead.'

I felt Christopher's feelings shift from shock to sadness, but I brushed them away. Christopher's hand landed on my shoulder and he pulled my gaze away from Euan.

'Why are you stopping me?' he said desperately. 'If they do this you'll have Rhys and Mikhail back. Isn't that what you want? I thought you of all people would understand what I'm doing here.'

'No!' I shouted at him. 'I want Rhys back more than anything, but I wouldn't go back, because then I would lose so much more.'

'But you wouldn't know you lost that,' he argued.

'But I know I can live without Rhys,' I yelled. 'As much as I loved him, I've learnt to live without him.'

He paused, finally understanding. 'Who can't you live without?'

I was suddenly thrown backwards off my feet, landing painfully on my back. I groaned as I propped myself up. Adestria held Christopher against the wall, her hand in his chest, my guess wrapped around his heart.

'Stop,' I yelled.

Her head spun back to look at me. Her green eyes had a gold swirl in them, when I saw them at the lake they were pure green. She could see the future, she wasn't pure goddess.

'He tried to change history and it would have destroyed everything,' she shouted, not moving her hand.

'That's why you saved me,' I enquired.

'You dying caused more bad ripple effects than good,' she said, putting her focus back on Christopher.

He grunted in pain. She probably was tightening her grip on his heart.

'Look again,' I said, she looked back at me again. 'I've changed his mind.'

I watched in amazement as her eyes swirled with green and gold. She visibly relaxed, blinked, then removed her hand from Christopher's chest. He collapsed to the ground. Adestria took a step back from him and walked over to me, offering me her bloody hand. I took it and she helped me to my feet. I looked back at Raven and Lorna who were still kneeling on the ground.

'Make sure his mind stays changed,' Adestria threatened before disappearing in a bolt of lightning.

'Well, wasn't that exciting,' Euan said, clapping his hands. I turned back to him, glaring.

'With the legend you hold, I thought you'd be different,' Tristan said, eyeing me over.

'She was only that legend in an act of revenge,' Euan said before I could speak. 'Though I wonder, could you uphold your name without that darkness?'

I didn't answer.

He was asking the very question I'd been asking myself since Elphina had returned. Could I beat her without the darkness? I looked back into Euan's eyes and he knew he'd struck a nerve. He grinned at me before leaning back in his seat. I took a deep breath, ensuring my emotions were in check and hidden.

I walked over to Christopher, pulling him to his feet. Helping him walk we began heading for the doors. They closed by themselves.

'Now Miss De-Valentino,' Euan said smugly. 'That boy was just offering us his life.'

Lorna and Raven came and each took one of Christopher's arms. I turned and walked back to stand in front of Euan. I stared him down, silently threatening him to stop me from taking Christopher. He smirked at me, before sighing impatiently.

'Just one last question, my dear. Have you ever considered joining us? Working for the high powers within this establishment.'

'That's never going to happen,' I said firmly, without hesitation. I could have this power if I wanted, I could overrule them and take back my kingdom if I wanted to.

'We could bring him back for you,' Euan said.

'Who?' I asked, confused.

'Mikhail.'

I felt my heart jump with desire. It wanted to scream apologises to Mikhail. Sorry for cheating on him, sorry for never falling in love with him, sorry for not being everything he deserved.

I shook my head declining the offer.

'I would offer you Rhys,' Euan said, slumping in defeat. 'But unfortunately his soul is not accessible to us.'

I wanted to ask what he meant, but turned away and started walking towards the doors which had reopened again. Lorna and Raven had already carried Christopher out. My nails were digging into my palms, threating to make me bleed.

As I reached the door I heard Euan's voice. 'Remember Arya, don't turn your back on your magic. Reliving the legend might be the only way to destroy Elphina.'

I stopped in my tracks for a moment before I continued walking. I would prove them wrong. I reached the centre of the crossroads and found Raven and Lorna waiting with Christopher for me.

'Meet me at home,' I said, not looking at any of them.

Lorna went to ask what I was going to do but I gave her a look, telling her I'd explain later. I watched as they continued down the hall and out the front door.

I looked down the hall that led to the Nagual. As I walked down it, I felt fear and excitement of what I was about to do and ask. I opened the door slowly, rather than burst in like I did to the last room. Ruby and Samuel were there wrestling in their cat forms. When I closed the door behind me they both stopped and looked in my direction. Samuel turned back into his human self. His handsome, devil-may-care demeanour caught me by surprise. He ruffled his already messy, brunette hair, his golden eyes studied me with curiosity. I turned away as he stood up to robe himself. He then sat beside Ruby again. He scratched Ruby's ears and she purred in gratitude.

'Hello kitten,' he said casually as I approached them.

Ruby growled at me before laying down beside Samuel, her head over his leg, eyeing me with caution.

'I know you don't owe me anything,' I said, now looking at Samuel, 'but I've come to ask a favour.'

He tilted his head, smiling at me, but he didn't say anything.

'My Lord,' I said, realising I should have put that in the sentence.

He laughed. 'Yes kitten, ask away. It does not mean I will grant it.'

'I want five minutes with Rhys,' I said.

He regarded me with curiosity again. I didn't know if I should keep eye contact or look away as he attempted to read my mind and soul imprint. I saw his eyes fall on the tattoo on my wrist. I looked down at my tattoo and over to his. It was the same, not that that surprised me.

'The Witches would be more likely to grant this wish,' he said, looking away.

'I know you can do it,' I said, taking another step forward.

Ruby stood up and transformed, stretching like a cat in human form. She flicked her hair forward to cover her breast before sitting back on her legs, her long dark hair falling in curls to her stomach. She ran her fingers over her lips as she smirked at me. I noticed even in human form she kept her feline teeth and nails.

'We'll grant this wish for you on one condition,' Ruby purred, stretching her arms above her head.

Samuel looked at her with confusion, which concerned me. I nodded to her, agreeing to this.

'I will give you one minute with Rhys, in exchange for you being powerless for fifteen minutes,' she said with a sadistic smile.

'When would I be powerless for fifteen minutes?' I asked.

She pressed her finger to her lips, stating that was only for her to know. I resisted the urge to roll my eyes and held my hand out to her, making the deal. She shook my hand and then transformed back into a cat. Rhys suddenly materialised behind them. I ran around them and threw my arms around Rhys's neck and kissed him, catching him by surprise.

'I love you,' I said, when I let him go.

He smiled at me. 'I wished you'd worked that out earlier. You're a kaleidoscope of hidden colours. Why must you keep them all within you?'

I shook my head, smiling at him. 'Are you happy?' I asked, my voice shaking.

'I am,' he said with a genuine smile. 'I want you to be happy too. You're alive, Arya. Live… for me.'

He began to fade under my fingertips. 'I love you, more than anything.'

'I'm just a memory,' he managed to let slip before disappearing.

I turned back to Ruby and Samuel to find only Samuel watching me. I looked around and found it was only the two of us in the room.

'Where is Ruby?' I demanded.

He shrugged.

'What did he mean he was just a memory?' I asked.

'Rhys's soul isn't available so she gave you a memory of what he was and who you wanted to see.'

'She tricked me,' I snapped.

When was she planning on stealing my powers? Fifteen minutes powerless could be dangerous in my world.

# CHAPTER THIRTY-FIVE

When I appeared home in a cloud of smoke I found Lorna, Raven and Christopher all sitting on the couch waiting for me.

'Where were you?' Lorna asked.

'I needed to say goodbye to Rhys,' I said, not meeting her eye contact.

Christopher stood and walked over to me. I slapped him and yelled at him for being so stupid, but then hugged him, slightly glad he was still alive. Raven laughed under her breath at me.

A fire note appeared before me. I released Christopher and caught it. I opened it and recognised Styr's handwriting.

*Elphina is waiting on the cliff for you.*

I folded the note and walked to the front door. Christopher grabbed my arm to stop me. I knew he'd read the note over my shoulder.

'You can't go,' Christopher urged. 'I'm sorry. Just stay here with me. You left me once before when you left on that dragon. Don't leave me again.'

'I won't ever be with you, Christopher,' I said, pulling away from him. I opened the front door.

'Why not?' he asked, sounding defeated.

I paused in the doorway. 'Because I promised Rhys,' I said before walking out the door and heading to the cliff.

As I reached the cliff, I put a shield up around me, hoping it'd make it harder for her to sense me. When she came into my sight I was glad to see she didn't know I was here yet. She was still looking over the cliff, waiting.

'What do you want?' I asked coldly, dropping my shields.

Elphina spun around, throwing webs at me, but I ducked them and threw a fireball at her, hitting her arm, causing her to howl in pain. She sneered at me, glad to see I was finally where she wanted me, well almost. Christopher ran up to me out of the forest. He tried to step in front of me but I pushed him to the side and hissed at him. He looked taken aback when he looked at me, and I knew my eyes were black.

'Finally,' Elphina snarled, throwing another web at me.

Again I dodged it and threw a bolt of electricity at her. I felt her screams through my body as the electricity ran through her. Christopher threw me to the ground, breaking my spell. Elphina took the moment to catch her break.

'Arya, please don't do this. I love you,' he begged.

'She deserves it,' I hissed. 'And what we had was never love. It was indiscretion and lust.'

He flinched at my words. 'I'm sorry.'

'Dammit, Christopher,' I yelled, causing storm clouds to darken the sky above. 'Stop saying you're sorry.' My eyes faded back to blue.

As Christopher walked off, I saw Ethan standing there watching the scene. His eyes went from me to Elphina. He went to take a step forwards but I growled, stopping him. Yes, he deserved revenge, but she was mine.

I turned around in time to see Elphina stand up, throwing webs at me which I deflected easily. I pulled the titanium blade out of my boot.

'Recognise this?' I said mockingly, standing over her. 'It's the same blade you killed Mikhail with, tried to kill me with and it's what I killed you with the first time.'

She snarled, noticing my eyes were no longer black. 'I don't care if I kill the legend or not, I just want your head.'

She leapt at me. I kept blocking her attacks, her nails threatening to slash my skin. She took a small step back and I saw an opening like the first time. I pushed the knife right through her heart, and like last time I watched her body fall to the ground after pulling the blade out.

'I'm not sorry,' I said, as I turned around to face Ethan.

He just walked up to me and kissed me. I kissed him back, dropping the knife at our feet. It was finally over, for both of us. We were free.

'I have to go fill Lorna in with what happened,' I said, breaking away from the kiss.

He kissed my lips quickly again. 'Then come to mine tonight, to celebrate,' he said with a wink before walking off. I smiled at his back.

I walked home, feeling exhilarated. I proved Euan wrong and it was finally over; the revenge, the pain. I could finally move on freely. I walked over the bridge back into town, breathing in the fresh air.

'Did you ever love him?' said a voice from behind me. I turned to see Raven standing on the bridge.

I shrugged. She looked away from me to take a deep breath. Muttered her thanks then walked off. She'd seen me reject him twice and leave him twice for a fight. Is that why I couldn't fall in love? The passion to fight was too strong within me.

When I walked in the front door, Lorna jumped off the couch and ran over to me. My parents looked up from the table confused at Lorna's enthusiasm. She mustn't have filled them in. I walked over to the table and stood before them.

'Mum, Dad,' I said, taking a swallow, 'Elphina got resurrected and tried to kill me, but I killed her first, without magic. It's over. Rhys's death has finally got justice.'

Mum jumped out of her chair and hugged me. I felt her fighting tears as she held me. Dad stood up and patted my back the way fathers do to say good job. I hugged Mum harder, resisting tears of my own.

I broke free and Lorna and I went up to my room and lay on my bed.

'Who are you going to choose?' she asked. 'Both Ethan and Christopher seem to be interested in you, but I can't tell who you're interested in.'

'Neither,' I said without hesitation.

'What are you going to do with your future?' Lorna said mockingly. She was hearing all about the future and such in high school since it was nearing end of senior year.

'We're going to leave. We are going to move to Kirravigne together and start anew.'

She hugged me before walking out of the room. I was originally thinking of moving alone, but Lorna's company would be much needed.

I heard arguing from outside. I went to the window and saw Mum and a red headed woman. She looked familiar. She flicked her hair back and I caught sight of her eyes, malicious yellow eyes. I recognised those eyes. They'd spoken to me in my dreams. Suddenly I noticed her tattoo. She was a Nagual, but she had a different scent; something sinister surrounded her.

'You know the prophecy, Nefertiti,' the woman purred. 'When she escapes a true form of darkness it will consume another soul until your bloodline is corrupted.'

'That's enough, Veronica,' yelled my father, who walked out of the house. I'd never seen my father yell. He looked so mad.

'Hello brother,' she smirked at him.

Nefertiti took my father's hand, they both glared at her. She held her hands up in defeat, smirking at them, glancing up at me, winking before turning around and walking away. I quickly stepped away from the window so my parents wouldn't see me.

What was that about?

I snuck downstairs to the front door to confront my parents when I noticed a letter with my name. I opened it and pulled out three pieces of paper. The first one read:

> *Don't think about leaving town.*
> *We'll be back. Kirstin + Daniel*

The other two were newspaper articles. One was of the attack behind the bar, my crime. The next was from today, two boys missing – Matt and Logan. I dropped the papers onto my bed and ran down to Lorna's room.

'We have to get to Matt and Logan's houses now,' I demanded.

Seeing my urgency she followed me out of the room. I told her to go to Logan's house and I teleported to the end of Matt's street and ran down to his house.

When I reached it, I saw a cop talking to his mum who was on her knees crying. I ran over and asked her what happened.

An hour later, I got back home and found Lorna waiting for me on the front porch. I sat beside her.

'They found Logan's body. He was mauled by a wolf,' she said, her eyes puffy and red from crying.

'Matt's body wasn't found. He's probably been turned into a werewolf.'

'How'd you know about this?' Lorna asked.

I took her up to my room and showed her what had been in the envelope.

'What are you going to do?' she asked.

'We're still moving, but I'm going to find Matt first. Try to appeal to his humanity and hopefully avoid the Hunters.'

'And if he's lost his humanity?'

I looked at Lorna for a moment before looking away.

'Then I'll kill him,' I said without hesitation.

# CHAPTER THIRTY-SIX

It was past midnight and I was still lying in bed wide awake. Why couldn't I sleep? I got up, staying in my pyjamas, and walked into the forest. My emerald green night dress brushed against my skin from the breeze; my hair blew around my face and neck, making me constantly brush it out of my face. I walked deep into the forest, away from my house. Following the leaves down until I got to the river. I looked across the water and saw Euan watching me with a smirk on his face.

'What are you doing here?' I asked.

'To congratulate you,' he said. 'You relived the legend without being consumed. You also don't have to worry about burying her bones this time. There's no possible way to resurrect her this time.'

I relaxed slightly out of relief, then tensed again, remembering who I was with.

'Why are you really here?'

Euan turned serious. 'I'm here to remind you, under our law you are not to kill your kind without good reason. Revenge isn't one of those reasons.'

I smirked at him. 'That's cute, that you think you control me,' I said, my old cockiness returning to my voice. 'If I wish it, I'll rule again. You can't touch me, and you can't condemn me for those I have killed, for reasons which are my own and good enough for me.'

He glared at me before disappearing.

As I turned around a fire note appeared before me. I opened it, and read it:

*Rhys is alive – Samuel*

# CHARACTERS

***The Rising Queens:***

| | |
|---|---|
| Ariella | Heir to Alesmera |
| Arya | Heir to Illyragasia |
| Adestria | Heir to Mycenae |
| Illyria | Heir to Meradom |
| Ekaterina | Heir to Underland |

**Introduced in Lost Worlds**

***Witches:***

| | |
|---|---|
| Tatiana Hale | Formerly in Cassandra Atlanta's coven |
| Yvette | Formerly in Cassandra Atlanta's coven, known enemy of Jareth |
| Aurora Atlanta | Cassandra Atlanta's younger sister |
| Cassandra Atlanta | Ariella's mother, Aubrey's wife (deceased) |
| Jessica | Chantelle and Jay's mother, enemies with Ariella since high school |
| Chantelle | High school friends of Ariella, but betrayed her once in Alesmera |
| Jay | High school friends of Ariella, but betrayed her once in Alesmera |
| Jareth | Aubrey's son, Ariella's half-brother, possibly heir to the throne, Arya's ex |
| Aubrey | Ariella's father, Cassandra's husband, King of Alesmera |
| Zed Hale | Tatiana's son, Ariella's boyfriend |
| Jesminda | Hale's ex fiancée |
| Adriana | Tatiana's daughter, Zed Hale's younger sister |

*Humans:*

| | |
|---|---|
| William Castle | Aurora's boyfriend, doctor |
| Serena | Ariella's neighbour and friend |
| Jordan | Ariella's friend |
| Eva | Ariella's friend |
| Colt | Used to work for Jareth, now Ariella's head guard |

*Gatekeeper:*

| | |
|---|---|
| Styr | Gatekeeper to pathways around Azriel, can communicate with living or dead |

*Elves:*

| | |
|---|---|
| Jace | Helps Ariella when she first arrives in Alesmera |
| Nancy | Helps Ariella, seeks a favour in return to rescue her sister |
| Lydia | Nancy's sister |

*Animals:*

| | |
|---|---|
| **Samir** | Black cat |
| **Laszlo** | Fox |

*Vampires:*

| | |
|---|---|
| Dom | Lives in Casa De Los Muertos |
| Julius Fleetwood | Lives in Casa De Los Muertos, fancies Ariella |
| Quinn | Soulless, in Unclaimed Lands, kidnapped Lydia |

*Sirens:*

| | |
|---|---|
| Lilith | Lives in Casa De Los Muertos, has a relationship with Arya |
| Margo | Lives in Casa De Los Muertos |
| Elena | Lives in Casa De Los Muertos |

**Introduced in Colours Within**

## *Witches:*

Lorna                     Arya's best friend

## *Nagual:*

Rhys                      Arya's brother **(deceased)**
Raiyn                     Arya's brother
Lorelei                   Raiyn's girlfriend
Archer                    Arya, Rhys, Raiyn & Lorelei's dad, Nefertiti's husband
Veronica                  Archer's sister
Ruby                      Oldest existing Nagual
Samuel                    Oldest existing Nagual

## *Elves:*

Nefertiti                 Arya, Rhys, Raiyn & Lorelei's mum, Archer's wife

## *Vampires:*

Jedhail                   Jackson family, Elphina's lover, Arya's enemy
Christopher               Jackson family, Arya's lover
Raven                     Jackson family
Echo                      Jackson family, Jarret's partner
Jarret                    Jackson family, Echo's partner
Ashard                    Jackson family, Laney's partner
Laney                     Jackson family, Ashard's partner
Ethan                     Deandray brother, very old and powerful
Tyler                     Deandray eldest brother, very old and powerful
Euan                      Oldest existing Vampire
Tristian                  Oldest existing Vampire
Orlando                   Oldest existing Vampire

*Humans:*

| | |
|---|---|
| Daniel Woodsen | Wyatt Hunter |
| Matthew | School friend |
| Logan | School friend |
| Kirstin | School friend |
| Missy | School friend |
| Aaron Malcolm | Jedhail's blood bonded human |

*Demons:*

| | |
|---|---|
| Mikhail | Arya's fiancé |
| Elphina | Jedhail's lover |
| Hecate | Controls souls and life and death |

# Acknowledgements

*'Imagination is the only weapon in the war against reality'*
*– Cheshire Cat*

Since I was a child, writing has been a passion of mine, and as I grew up it became an outlet. For as long as I can remember my friends and family have shown me nothing but support, and the reviews they gave me from my first book was overwhelming and I thank you all so much.

I want to thank my Dad, my Mum and my brother, Riley. Thank you for not waking me up when I'd stay up till the early hours of the morning writing and always believing that I could do this. I love you.

Thank you to all my crazy but amazing family, you have always been so supportive of my dreams, you've always asked me how my writing is going and encouraging me.

Thank you to my amazing friends and family friends who have always been so supportive towards me.

A big shout out to my Alice in Wonderland girls and Twisted Sister, you know who you are. I could not have got this far without you in my life, you guys are my rock, love you all forever.

Thank you to Phoenix and Sabrina for the edits of Book Two. I really appreciate all the feedback, and the time you took to edit my work. Thank you so much!! I'm sorry if the early drafts were slightly painful.

Wayne, thank you for another amazing cover! I am so glad I found you, I don't think any other artist could draw what I have in my mind, especially with the very bad descriptions and attempted drawings of what I want.

A shout out to all my fellow authors who have given me advice, especially Kimberley and Jacinta, I hope to build amazing friendships out of these experiences.

Cover design by Wayne Nichols
www.wnichols.com

Map by Amber Morant
www.ambermorant.com

Find us at
www.facebook.com/ouroborusbooks
and
www.facebook/danicapecknovels

Enjoy a sneak peek at Danica's upcoming book

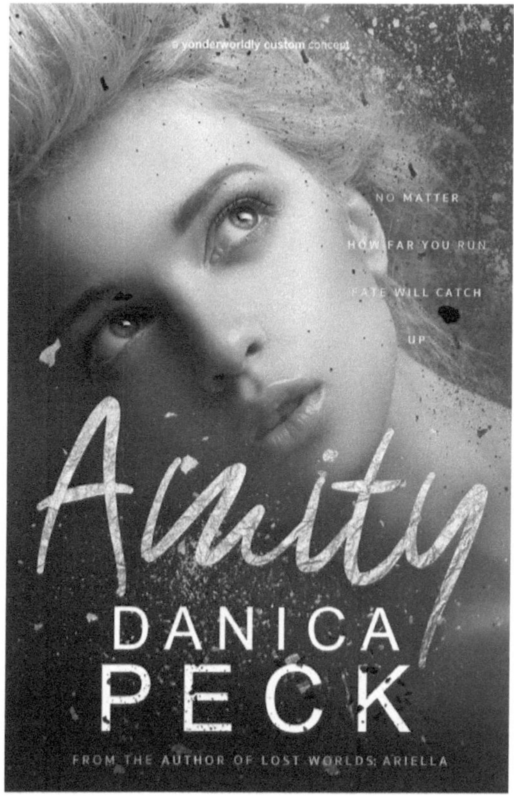

# CHAPTER ONE

## AMITY

I've been running for seven years, running from the heartbeat in my chest, ignoring dreams and memories that wandered into my mind, avoiding the emotions that plague my soul. No matter how far I ran I couldn't escape them, because they weren't mine. These things I was so desperate to outrun belonged to my bond mate, I felt his heart in my chest, I felt his laughter, his sadness, his need for me.

I'm from a world that isn't like yours. Miriam is a world where your choice is taken from you when you bond with someone. We are all born with grey eyes, very simple. When we bond they change colour.

If they go blue you work with the boats, and make sure no one tries to step foot on the island. Miriam is one large island where everyone lives, except us runaways who find smaller islands that aren't civilised.

If they go golden you work on the farms, to collect food and care for the animals.

If they go green you go into the ruling system to govern the people.

If they go red you're a warrior.

If your eyes remain grey you stay in the village where our parents retire and people return to when on leave from their responsibilities.

If they go purple, you're an outcast. Cursed. An abomination. It means you are dangerous.

When I bonded, my eyes went purple.

To make the situation worse, I bonded with the town leader's youngest son, Wes DeLaurentis. It was rumoured that if you left your bond mate, your eyes would fade back to grey. That is why I left; unfortunately my eyes remained purple. I had seen Wes through his eyes when he looked into a mirror; his had gone back to grey, which pleased me.

I now stood on a cliff in Thira, staring out at the ocean, a war waging in my mind over whether I should go home. The previous night, I had been in a small tavern when whispers reached my ear; whispers that Nicholas DeLaurentis had been killed. Should I head home to say my goodbyes and perhaps avenge him, or stay away, because the minute I returned home to Miriam, Wes's eyes would turn purple again, and his heartbeat would be even stronger in my chest.

Melina nudged her nose into my back, so I turned away from the ocean and wrapped my arms around her neck. Melina was my Pegasus, a horse with the wings of a bird. Though, Melina was a rare breed, her body was the colour and had the stripes of a tiger, her tail was as red as a sunset, and her wings as black as night. Never had anyone seen a Pegasus like her. When I first ran away, she saved me when my boat had been shipwrecked and I had almost died.

We'd been together ever since.

'You're going to go to him, aren't you?' said a deep voice.

Releasing my hold of Melina's neck, I met Lucian's gaze. His dark eyes studied me. I shrugged and turned away to look over the ocean again. Lucian was a centaur; his horse part was a chestnut colour and his body was tanned and toned. Even though he was half man, he was stronger, physically and mentally than any human I had ever met.

'Remember, I don't need a bond to read someone's thoughts,' he said, as he came and stood beside me on the cliff.

I looked sideways at him, but his gaze was now fixated on the ocean. We had spent many hours up on this cliff, him training me to survive and embrace the colour of my eyes, rather than fear them.

'Was it your bond mate that died?' he asked, looking at me.

Shaking my head, I looked away again.

'His brother.'

I could feel Lucian's gaze studying me.

'How come I feel that your loss of this one is more powerful than that felt because of the distance of your bond mate?'

Turning back to meet his gaze, I felt numb. 'Nicholas and I were close, inseparable. Wes and I didn't know each other that well. I don't understand why I was bonded with him.'

'Fate is a funny thing, but she does everything for a reason. Maybe if you go back you'll learn this reason.'

I ran my finger back through my silver and purple hair. My cheeks felt rosy from the cold, though that was the most colour my skin ever had, I was fair skinned. I wore dark blue jeans and a loose black shirt.

Lucian always lectured me about my wardrobe, because I literally had five outfits. The one I wore now, a short white summer dress, my grey battle armour, a travelling cloak, and a pale purple floor length night gown.

That's all I carried, along with my weapons and supplies. I always kept my possessions in a bag with me, ready to run again if I needed to. Melina and this small black duffle bag was all I needed to survive.

'Tell me what to do, Lucian,' I said, as the war continued within my mind.

Lucian watched a few more waves crash into the bottom of the cliff before turning his attention back to me.

'You are my greatest achievement, and I will be sad to lose you.'

Melina neighed and pawed the ground from behind me. Apparently, everyone but me knew the decision was made. Why was it so hard for me to admit to myself that I needed to go home?

'Have you ever been in love?' I asked Lucian, like I do every time I think of Nicholas and Wes.

In seven years, he never answered me but told me to keep training.

'Yes,' he said after a pause, surprising me. 'Fate took her away from me.'

'I'm sorry,' I whispered, regretting asking him, all those times I forced him to remember her.

He shook his head, 'I'm not anymore. The place she died is where I found you, and yes, the loss of her still hurts, but finding you and the friendship we built healed a lot of my wounds.'

Without thinking I threw my arms around his neck and hugged him. In seven years, this was the first time I'd ever hugged him. He wrapped his arms around me after the shock of what I'd done had worn off.

'Promise this isn't goodbye,' he whispered.

'I promise,' I replied before stepping out of the hug. 'When this is all over, I will come back. I will never be accepted back home.'

'I will miss you, Amity Winters,' he said before winking at me, then I watched as he turned and galloped down the hill.

Letting out a deep breath, I turned back to Melina. I mounted her and as we stood on the edge of the cliff, I breathed in the sea air.

'Take me home,' I whispered, my voice sounding braver than I felt inside.

Melina neighed in response before neighing and taking flight off the cliff's edge.